I0720770

REBEL ON THE RUN

JAYNE RYLON

Copyright © 2014 by Jayne Rylon

All rights reserved. No part of this book may be used or reproduced in any manner whatsoever without written permission from the author, except in the case of brief quotations used in reviews.

This book is a work of fiction. The names, characters, places, and incidents are products of the writer's imagination or have been used fictitiously and are not to be construed as real. Any resemblance to persons, living or dead, actual events, locale or organizations is entirely coincidental.

eBook ISBN: 978-1-941785-37-9
Print ISBN: 978-1-941785-69-0

Ebook Cover Art By Angela Waters
Print Book Cover Art By Jayne Rylon
Interior Print Book Design By Jayne Rylon

Sign Up For The Naughty News!
Contests, sneak peeks, appearance info, and more.
www.jaynerylon.com/newsletter

Shop
Autographed books, reading-themed apparel,
notebooks, totes, and more.
www.jaynerylon.com/shop

Contact Jayne
Email: contact@jaynerylon.com
Website: www.jaynerylon.com
Facebook: Facebook.com/JayneRylon
Twitter: @JayneRylon

OTHER BOOKS BY JAYNE RYLON

<u>DIVEMASTERS</u>
Going Down
Going Deep
Going Hard

<u>MEN IN BLUE</u>
Night is Darkest
Razor's Edge
Mistress's Master
Spread Your Wings
Wounded Hearts
Bound For You

<u>POWERTOOLS</u>
Kate's Crew
Morgan's Surprise
Kayla's Gift
Devon's Pair
Nailed to the Wall
Hammer it Home

HOTRODS

King Cobra
Mustang Sally
Super Nova
Rebel on the Run
Swinger Style
Barracuda's Heart
Touch of Amber
Long Time Coming

COMPASS BROTHERS

Northern Exposure
Southern Comfort
Eastern Ambitions
Western Ties

COMPASS GIRLS

Winter's Thaw
Hope Springs
Summer Fling
Falling Softly

PLAY DOCTOR

Dream Machine
Healing Touch

<u>**STANDALONES**</u>
4-Ever Theirs
Nice & Naughty
Where There's Smoke
Report For Booty

<u>**RACING FOR LOVE**</u>
Driven
Shifting Gears

<u>**RED LIGHT**</u>
Through My Window
Star
Can't Buy Love
Free For All

<u>**PARANORMALS**</u>
Picture Perfect
Reborn
<u>**PICK YOUR PLEASURES**</u>
Pick Your Pleasure
Pick Your Pleasure 2

DEDICATION

For Amanda Hicks in appreciation of her competitive spirit. For the record, I did kick your ass in the inflatable obstacle course, but I applaud your effort and respect the scar you bear as proof of how insanely tough that wobbly wall climb really was. Plus, you definitely won when it came to style points since—unlike me—you finished still wearing your pants when you came down the final giant slide. Rematch, anytime!

CHAPTER ONE

Kaelyn DuChamp kicked the flat tire of her Maserati then hopped around, cursing her likely broken toe. The heel of her stiletto stuck in the mushy ground. A half-dozen windmills of her arms couldn't stop her from face-planting. On the bright side, the field her car had careened to a stop in *was* lush. Spitting blades of grass from between her teeth, she attempted to dust off the skirt of her Chanel suit. No use.

When she spotted long, streaked stains on the periwinkle silk, she surrendered to the will of the universe. She flopped onto her back in the wildflower-dotted meadow, trying to appreciate the late-summer blooms and the cotton-candy clouds overhead. An insect of some sort skittered across her thigh. Without looking, she pretended it was a ladybug, since with her luck it probably was a tarantula. Or a millipede. Definitely something poisonous.

Aaaacccckkk.

Forget communing with nature. She should have stayed in the sweltering car. After two hours baking while staring at her dead phone, she'd thought maybe she should try to expand her horizons. Nope. Never mind.

Good thing there was no one within a five-mile radius of her crash site, on the fringe of a podunk town. Her awkward slapping and lurching would have convinced a passerby she was having a seizure.

Somehow, Kaelyn ended up on her knees. Butt on her heels—one shoed, one not—she searched frantically for bugs or snakes or Bigfoot or whatever the heck else might be lurking in the vegetation surrounding her. The bucolic landscape now felt ominous instead of serene, as it had appeared while she coasted past, singing along to the radio in a failed attempt at levity. Her heart pounded as she considered crawling onto the backseat of her busted ride and taking a nap instead of exploring to alleviate her boredom. At least sleep might take her mind off the thirst that had turned her mouth into a fair imitation of the Sahara desert in the couple hours since her tire had detonated.

Why hadn't she packed a bottle of water?

This is what happened when you tried to fly free.

Who was she kidding? A caged bird like her would never cut it in the wild.

Kaelyn took a deep breath. Then another. Life beyond the invisible crystal bars on her not-so-perfect mansion windows might not be as carefree and exhilarating as she'd imagined while trapped inside, strangled by miles of bureaucracy and endless decorum. Both of which had been unpleasant inheritances bestowed on her as the daughter of an aristocratic politician.

Well, crap.

At least the creepy guy who'd tried to lure her into his pickup a while ago had left with a promise to dispatch a tow truck. Though disgustingly dirty, his ride hadn't seemed nearly as soiled as his oily leers when he'd invited her to tag along rather than wait for roadside assistance.

She figured the chances of him pocketing the last of her cash without a glance in his rearview mirror had to be at least fifty-fifty.

Proud of her vanishing naiveté, Kaelyn still regretted her recently tarnished outlook on the universe. She sighed. The deep inhale that followed sucked pollen into the far reaches of her lungs. A sneeze ripped through her. It loosened more hair from her usual chignon, flinging platinum tendrils into her face.

She might have addressed the mess if the rumble of an engine hadn't caught her attention. Hobbling on mismatched legs—one now five inches shorter than the other—toward the road, she waved her arms and bounced like an insane castaway who'd been stranded on a deserted island for a decade.

Her effort wasn't necessary. Flashing amber lights crested the hill, followed by a monstrous tow truck decked out in chrome and metallic onyx paint. Enormous fireball graphics exploded over the hood, as if the vehicle plowed through an inferno. Its driver seemed proportionally huge behind the wheel. Either that or the company had a grizzly bear for a mascot and allowed the thing to respond to emergencies.

Darn. Please don't let this guy be sketchy too, she prayed.

A lifetime of etiquette instruction took control and Kaelyn attempted to groom her disheveled hair, fix her suit, haul her shoe from the muck and school her face into a calm mask of indifference all at once. Illusions were the only source of power she had left.

Instead she only managed to turn in circles, put some color in her cheeks and propel her heart rate from elevated to a ridiculous, extra-nervous thumping that pulsed in her fingertips while she began to perspire.

Fantastic.

Kaelyn deflated, admitting to herself that her great escape had more in common with a fledgling tumbling out of a nest than a majestic eagle learning to spread its wings and soar. She stared at the long, broad shadow her unlikely savior cast as he rounded the hood of his behemoth machine. *Please, let him be decent.*

Did such people exist? She wouldn't bet on it anymore.

The clomp of his boots on the tar and gravel of the road was sure and steady as he ate up the distance between them with the immense length of his strides. Laying her shaky, sweaty palms against her thighs, she forced herself to lift her chin.

Kaelyn prepared to do something she rarely did. Okay, *never* had done before.

Ask for help.

Beg for charity from a stranger no less. Humbling.

Usually she was the one organizing benefits for those less fortunate.

Except, when she scanned from his leather boots to his ripped jeans, which hugged his tree-trunk thighs, to a grease-stained T-shirt that showcased his impressive chest and broad shoulders, everything she'd rehearsed—about how she'd work off her debt, or leave an IOU behind—stuck in her throat.

Or maybe that lump was her heart.

Heaven knew that worthless thing had stopped cold.

Because her savior seemed awfully familiar. He was what her best friend might have looked like if she'd seen the kid grow into an unapologetically sexy man. Instead, his rebellious teenaged urges had led him to a life roaming Europe as some reclusive rich playboy, who'd forgotten about the girl next door by the time his father's private jet touched down across the pond. She glanced at her inherited Maserati and swallowed around the pain that still lanced her when she indulged in memories of Bryce Ellington IV.

If he hadn't abandoned her, maybe everything could have been different.

Wishful thinking, she knew from endless experience, didn't change what had happened. But it could ease the pain for a moment. She thought of him—drawing on the strength he'd embodied before he'd gone completely selfish—to get her through this, like other rough times.

It must be a sign that this man was Bryce's spitting image. Part of her relaxed.

Unfortunately, she must have whispered his name.

And that's when the world went insane.

"Yeah, Kae. It's me." The grim set of his mouth didn't make him seem happy to see her. "I thought maybe you wouldn't recognize me. It's been so long. And I'm...a hell of a lot different. But, I'm not going to lie. Part of me is glad you haven't forgotten."

It was the twinkle in his steely eyes that proved the impossible things spilling from this not-stranger's wicked mouth. Surely, his rough and rugged exterior had nothing in common with the groomed adolescent she'd known. Still, something unmistakable reached out and grabbed her.

"*Bryce*?" she croaked again. Louder this time. It felt rusty rolling off her tongue. Confusion had her lids fluttering as she struggled to believe what she saw. Completely overwhelmed, she blinked up at him. Squinted. Scrubbed her eyes.

The vision remained.

This was no rich, idle son. No, he was a blue-collar sex god right here in the US of freaking A. Forget another continent, she'd found him less than two states away. What happened to the stories his father had told her of Bryce's escapades with an endless stream of gorgeous foreign women, with whom she could never compare?

Was nothing she believed the truth?

"Hi." He reached toward her when the periphery of the world turned black, though he paused as if to admire her, unaware of the way things melted into a Dali-scape in her vision. "Damn. You grew up fine, didn't you?"

She might have offered some witty remark if her entire mouth hadn't gone numb along with the rest of her body. It wasn't every day she saw the ghost of BFFs past.

"Shit!" He jogged, closing the gap between them with a couple giant strides, his arms outstretched to brace her.

Kaelyn retreated, afraid to let him touch her. This couldn't be happening.

"But you're gone!" she shrieked as she stumbled backward.

"I'm not. I never really left the country." He winced as she wondered if he could be some kind of imposter. "Who else would know about the times we snuck over to your tree house and camped out, spending the summer nights looking at the stars and telling each other about our dreams? Or the stray cat we made our pet out there? Remember the time you snuck Mr. Whiskers that fancy salmon from your dad's Christmas party?"

"Bryce? Is this some sick trick my father is playing?" Anything made more sense than what this impersonator spouted.

"No, Kae." He swallowed hard. "It's really me."

"I see." She'd never punched a person in her life. Yet her fingers bunched before she could stop them. Next thing she knew, she had risen onto her tiptoes and decked him in his handsome, though no longer clean-shaven, jaw. The bristle of his whiskers chafed her skin as his face and her fist collided.

"Christ!" He clutched the spot her hand had bounced off of, injuring her knuckles in the process. "What was that for?"

"If you're here, you're a big fat liar." Steam had built within her in a flash. Now vented, she sagged under the relieved pressure. "I don't understand. Why? I cried buckets when your dad told me you'd gone to enjoy your freedom. That you'd left without bothering to say goodbye. That you didn't plan to come home because there was nothing important for you there. That you were enjoying the high life, the parties, the *women.* And here you are, six hours from Windsor...driving a *tow truck*? This is crazy. The whole world is flipping nuts."

Whether it was because of dehydration, the shock or the devastation at discovering her supposed best friend's ultimate betrayal—or maybe all of those factors together—Kaelyn felt as though she were watching herself from a distance.

"Hey. I'm actually a mechanic. The truck is..." Bryce trailed off, probably spotting her glazed eyes. He lunged for her again, attempting to steady her as she listed to the left. "Are you okay? You look like you're going to pass—"

His concern became garbled as her eyelids grew heavy. Her knees buckled. At least the grass would make a soft landing pad, *again*, she thought.

Yet when she blinked against the bright sun swimming above, it didn't seem like much time had passed and she definitely wasn't sprawled on the ground. No, those were muscled arms cradling her against a very hard chest. One that had nothing in common with gentlemen she'd held at an appropriate distance while waltzing during her father's social functions. Or even the handful she'd invited to share her bed.

She attempted to protest, to keep herself separate from the guy she would have wanted—far too much—to come to her rescue if given a single wish. Though she'd figured it impossible. Maybe she'd hit her head when her tire had blown. Maybe this was some sick trick of her mind, recalling the one person who'd always had her back when she needed him most. Except transformed into the kind of man who wouldn't place leisurely pursuits above hard work, dedication and loyalty.

That had to be it. He was a figment of her imagination.

Kaelyn reached way up and pinched his thick neck. Hard.

"Ouch! What the hell?" He glared at her.

A combination whimper and chuckle left her parched throat. She didn't know whether to laugh or cry. Both seemed imminent. The chaos in her mind had her yearning to black out again. So she surrendered. Kaelyn allowed herself to be weak and lean on Bryce as she'd longed to do so many times in his decade-long absence. "Making sure you're real."

"Come on, *your majesty*. Let me hoist your chariot onto the flatbed and we'll get the hell out of here. I'm taking you home."

"No! You can't make me go back." Despite the futility, she attempted to thrash and squirm from his unrelenting grip. "Please."

"Hush. Jesus! What has you so scared, Kae? I don't mean your father's house. I'm taking you to *my* place. Where you'll be safe. I swear. We can work out the rest later." Bryce didn't really give her a choice in the matter.

He made it easy to surrender, though she hated letting him take care of her. Right when she'd vowed to gain control of her life, her choices, her future. "Whatever has you freaked out, I'll take care of it. I promise I'll fix it. I'll—"

"Stop talking." Here she was, in the arms of another bastard who'd lied to her.

For her own good.

She must have growled against his neck—which smelled amazing, damn him.

When he chuckled, rumbling against her ear, she balled her fists and thumped them against his chest. A waste of effort. The ineffective blows rained over him without denting his resilient muscles. "Okay. Whatever it takes. Settle down."

She tried, but her newly honed survival instincts screamed at her to run.

He held her tighter. "I get that you're pissed. I didn't mean to laugh. But you always were adorable when you got mad. Some things never change, I guess."

Before she could lash out again, he shocked her by dropping a light kiss on her forehead.

"I missed you, Kae," he murmured. "Every fucking day."

"Could have fooled me." She would have crossed her arms over her chest if she'd been standing on her own. Both to protect herself from his charm and to hold in the jagged pieces of her soul. "You knew how to find me. And didn't."

"It's not that simple." He at least had the dignity to look away when he dug himself deeper into a nest of falsehoods. Concentrating on his steps, he toted her to his truck and shifted her to one side when he put his hand on the door handle.

"Why did you go? Your father knew? And mine?"

When he sighed but didn't deny it, she sagged.

"Why did they cover it up? Were they embarrassed you'd decided to work for a living? I think that's kind of...cool. You always loved tinkering with your car." She shook her head, hating to admit it. "Is everyone dishonest? How stupid have I been to believe them?"

Before Bryce could answer, a riot of yips boomed from the truck's cabin.

They would have knocked her on her butt if she'd approached on her own. Good thing Bryce cradled her as if he'd never drop her. Too bad she knew better than to believe in fairy tales like that anymore. She cringed, hating that it seemed she curled into his embrace instead of shrinking from the latest threat.

"Don't let that pup fool you. He's harmless. Annoyed 'cause I wouldn't let him run around like a maniac in these weeds." Bryce laughed again, deeper and more fully this time. Despite her anger and confusion and...*hurt*...the sound filled her with joy. Relief that her universe still held that lyrical resonance, and the man who made it, snowed her.

Though he'd betrayed their friendship and the bond she'd thought they had, it brought tears to her eyes to know that he was here. Happy. That he'd escaped from the world of politics and inhibitions they'd grown up in. Combined with the rest of the recent drama in her life, it was too much. She wilted, completely devoid of energy. She had nothing left to give. Wrung out and exhausted, she allowed Bryce to shoo his dog then set her on the seat of his massive truck.

The adorable mutt wagged his tail hard enough that he might have knocked himself over if he hadn't clambered into her lap and licked her face like it was some canine lollipop. His black and white markings, pointy ears and big brown eyes made her think of the Boston terrier Mrs. Winthorpe loved to bring along on equestrian outings.

"Smart dog." Bryce groaned. "Kae, this is Buster McHightops. Give me five minutes and I'll have us on our way."

Kaelyn couldn't help herself. She cracked a smile at the puppy's unconditional love. The animal, at least, was innocent. She patted his head and scratched behind his perky ears. Within minutes, he'd curled up in her lap, accepting her repetitive stroking, which helped to calm her mind as well.

In the side mirror, she admired Bryce's easy strength and sure movements as he went about his business. This was familiar territory for him. Comfortable in his impressive body, and at this job, he nearly had her drooling like Buster McHightops while she spied on him. Shaking her head to clear the desire fogging her righteous indignation, terror and—okay, fine—relief, she closed her eyes to block the sight.

Before he could return and ruin the first sliver of peace she'd managed to find since her world had imploded, she succumbed to the pretense of security. Even if it was false, she needed a break. A chance to regroup.

Because finding out yet another fact about her apparent life of unwitting lies might break her. The first few had cracked her. The man she glimpsed in the rearview mirror—sexy, strong and alluring—had the power to shatter her beyond repair.

He always had.

CHAPTER TWO

Bryce couldn't believe the way life worked sometimes. Almost as if masterminded by a freaking sadist.

He'd finally gotten his shit together. Buried his past. Dedicated himself to moving on as a self-invented man. Everything he had, he'd earned. The group of guys he'd grown up with and ran a prosperous business with— the Hot Rods—were building something he thought he could be satisfied with for the long haul. Professionally *and* personally.

A miracle in and of itself.

Business was booming. They'd been slammed the whole damn summer and had a mile-long waitlist for restomods. It grew each day thanks to Nola's new graphic proposals. Kaige's girlfriend had shaken things up. Advanced them. Evolved the whole shop. Both at the garage and on the home front.

The addition of Nova's lady brought a new layer to their already complex relationship, which had cemented some with Eli, Alanso and Sally's wedding. In a group of people who'd lived transient childhoods, the stability itself was welcome. Attractive.

And that was before he tallied how much being included in that sphere of love counted toward easing the knots that had been tied in his guts for years. Since he'd left Kaelyn.

The sexual sharing the seven guys and two women had done recently filled a void in Bryce, one he had long ago resigned himself to living with. At least once he'd realized no woman would replace in his heart the one he'd had to sacrifice more than a decade ago. He might not be part of a soul-mate pairing—like Eli, Alanso and Sally or Kaige and Nola—but those in their group who were made it clear that he and the rest of the unattached guys hadn't been left in their dust. In addition to the Hot Rods' friendship, which had lasted since Bryce had leeched Tom London's hospitality and moved in above the garage, he now had something...*more*.

They'd begun to explore the connection they'd formed, expanding their relationships beyond partners to lovers, forming a web of intersecting bonds that were complex and deceptively strong. Durable. A natural marvel.

Bryce had taken pleasure in delighting Mustang Sally or Nola with the knowledge he was giving to his fellow Hot Rods—their guys—in the process. Hell, he'd even started to look forward to messing around with Holden or Carver or whichever of his garagemates might be impatient to play when the ladies were otherwise occupied. Meep gave damn fine blowjobs. Enjoyed doing it too.

Who was Bryce to reject an offer like that?

Group sessions in their living room had become a regular occurrence. Something he anticipated. It helped ground him. Made him feel almost whole. Settled.

The Hot Rods' open-minded arrangement had been a lifesaving compromise, which he'd never dreamed possible. It allowed him to feel as if he hadn't betrayed the memory of the girl he'd pledged his soul to while granting himself some comfort. Non-traditional intimacy filled the emptiness within him. Dark loneliness had been eating him alive, rotting him from the inside out.

Finally, he had battled back.

Shit, these days he even had a dog. Sure, Buster McHightops was a tiny runt of a thing, not much to look at yet. But he was fierce. A survivor. He loved unconditionally. Like the rest of the gang. Speaking of the pup, he trailed hot on Bryce's heels, whining as if he could possibly be as concerned about the lady Bryce held as Bryce was himself.

Carrying Kaelyn DuChamp up the open-backed metal stairway to his home, he couldn't help but wonder how her presence would alter his future. Rock the foundation of his newly expanded happiness. There wasn't a question of if she would shift his course. No, it was more like *how much* she would bend his trajectory through this new life he'd created.

Because the woman he held was even more amazing than the girl he'd left behind.

Stunning. A fighter, yet vulnerable. He attempted to work the ache out of his jaw— both from clenching the damn thing and from where she'd bopped him—as he studied her lax features. Gorgeous. Though he wondered about the puffy redness of her face. Had she been crying? What had brought her out this way if she really hadn't known he was here? And why hadn't she had anyone to call for help when that damn tire blew?

He'd checked it quickly while loading the car on the flat bed. They were the same fucking set he'd put on the car himself, far too long ago for them to be road worthy.

He had to know more about the fear he'd glimpsed in Kae's eyes before shock had paralyzed her. It hadn't been entirely a product of seeing a man she'd thought long vanished that had derailed her from her usual patrician serenity. At least he didn't think so. His blood boiled at the thought of someone trying to hurt her. Fuck, hadn't he given up everything to keep her safe?

Like hell would someone threaten her now.

Maybe there was such a thing as fate after all.

In one morning, two worlds had collided. Bryce had yet to see through the glare to determine the damage that had been done. Even once they untangled the snarl of deceptions he'd perpetrated, how would she react if she found out about his new lifestyle?

Too many unanswered questions clogged his mind. The safe haven that grew closer with each step attracted him like a bug to a flickering neon light. With the help of the Hot Rods, they could fix this. He trusted the gang to make things right again. It was what they specialized in. Alanso, Sally and Kaige had each had recent run-ins with their pasts. Bryce refused to break their winning streak. He'd conquer his demons too. He hoped. The alternative was unacceptable. Raining danger on his pseudo-family wouldn't be tolerated.

Tom, the guys, Sally and Nola... People who cared would rally around him. Extending that same protection to Kaelyn would be second nature. Grateful as ever, he hoped that what they would learn about him today wouldn't change that fundamental tenant of his life. *Please don't let them kick me out.*

He couldn't survive without them. Maybe Kaelyn couldn't either, given her panic over going home.

For her, he'd come clean.

As he approached, the door to the apartment over the garage opened. Holden ushered him inside, peeking at Bryce's precious cargo.

"You brought me a present?" The smartass raised his brows. "She's a mega-hottie. Thanks."

But when the guy reached out, Bryce couldn't believe the overprotective instincts that roared to life. They had him turning away from his partner. "She's mine."

Uh-oh. Hot Rods didn't do possessive.

At least, not after a primary claim had been staked. Shock flashed across Holden's face before he stood back and held the door wider. "Got it. Bring in *your* girl. Everyone's here. Except Tom. We thought we should wait and see what was up before calling him over."

Swinger—nicknamed for the car he drove, like the rest of the Hot Rods—spoke loud and clear enough to transmit the message to the entire gang. Though they loved their surrogate dad, Eli's genetic father, they could tell by Bryce's earlier vanishing act that something was haywire. A sketchy guy had come into the shop today and described a stranded damsel so uniquely amazing, Bryce had immediately known who'd crash-landed in his backyard.

He'd hightailed it out of the garage to rescue her.

Alone.

It didn't take a genius to figure out she was a part of his past. One he didn't discuss with anyone, not even his mechanic family.

He tried not to meet their worried gazes as he came inside. Instead, he concentrated on depositing Kaelyn gently on the couch. Then he knelt on the floor beside her. Buster McHightops hopped onto the leather sectional and curled against her torso. When Bryce attempted to shoo the pup, he emitted a rare growl.

"Whoa." Bryce withdrew his hand in a hurry before his fingers got nipped by baby teeth capable of shredding a pair of thick leather work gloves in less time than it took to go zero to sixty in his Rebel AMC.

"Guess Buster thinks she's *his*." Holden clapped Bryce on the shoulder before taking a seat on the sofa, around the bend in the couch. "Maybe you should have peed on her. Marked your territory or some shit."

"Fuck you, Swinger." Bryce stared at his dog, not too upset since he liked the idea of Kaelyn having an ally. God knew she wouldn't count him as one once she realized how much of the history she thought she'd lived through had to be rewritten to be accurate.

Everyone gathered around gave him courage. He took a breath, prepared for her to despise him, then shook her shoulder gently. "Kae?"

"Bryce?" She fisted her hand.

"Yeah, it's me. And you already clocked me once when you realized I wasn't gallivanting around Europe, so you don't have to do it again." He grinned, since his jaw hadn't suffered much from her ineffectual punch.

Instead of hitting him, she rubbed her knuckles into her eyes, then blinked and took a second look. He figured it was a good sign when her gaze lingered on his mouth. "This isn't a dream? It wasn't a nightmare."

Her head flopped onto the throw pillow as she went limp again.

"*Europe*?" Eli—the garage's owner, their King Cobra—shuffled closer, speaking at the same time. "What's that about? Why would she think that?"

Bryce shook his head. "It's a load of bullshit my father told her. Kae and I knew each other when we were kids."

Damn if he hadn't done a helluva lot of growing up those last few years he'd spent with her. Too bad she'd been too young then. Too innocent for the thoughts he'd had of her. The desire. And too dependent to run rebel with him. Otherwise, life could have been so much better...

He swallowed hard, then looked at Kaelyn directly. "That boy is as good as dead. I'm not that person anymore. So if you came looking for him, I'm sorry. You're not gonna find him."

She seemed as though she might argue. Except when she parted those lush lips, a croak came out, followed by a wince.

Bryce leaned in to support her as she sat up, trying not to notice the elegant curve of her shoulder against his palm. "What hurts?"

He ran his hands along her arms, noting the gooseflesh that broke out in the wake of his rough fingers on her porcelain skin.

"Nothing physical." She glanced around the room, her gaze flitting to him, and his mouth, periodically. Though so many tough guys—tattoos and piercings galore showing beneath tanks or ripped jeans—hovering in a semi-circle had to be overwhelming for a sheltered, refined woman like her, she didn't cower. Instead she spoke, in a tone filled with husk. "I'll take the biggest glass of water you have, though. Please."

"You got it." Carver, closest to the kitchen, which sprawled open to the living area, trotted over and rummaged through a cabinet.

In the meantime, Kaelyn stared up at Bryce with enormous eyes. "I wasn't looking for you. I thought you were long gone. I still can't believe this is happening."

He held absolutely still as she cupped his cheek, her thumb caressing the stubble there. Her awe he could handle better than her ire. Though if she didn't stop eyeing him like she planned to lean in and kiss him hello, he might do the job for her.

"Okay, then what's going on?" he asked. "What brought you to Middletown?"

"Sorry. I'll tell you, I promise." Her scratchy whisper had Carver hurrying at the sink. "But who are these people?"

"Oh, crap. Um." Bryce pointed as he went around the room. "Guys, meet Kaelyn DuChamp. Kae, the bossman is Eli London. Hot Rods is his place, his and his father's. Tom's. Next to him are his husband and his wife. Alanso and Sally."

"Excuse me? I think I heard you wrong." Kaelyn shook her head as if to clear it.

"Nah, *chica*. You got it right. The three of us are a set." The bald Cuban man spoke for himself and his partners. "Nice to meet you, by the way."

Kaelyn blinked a few times but didn't object. She bestowed a hint of her brilliant smile. "Same here. You make a cute trio."

"Thanks." Sally grinned, then waved her fingers, showing off pretty pink-and-silver nails. "I think they're handsome fuckers myself."

"She was talking about you, Mustang." Eli kissed her on the forehead. The scorching gazes they exchanged might have led to something more, if the situation hadn't been so unusual and so serious.

Bryce hurried so he could hear her story. "Next to them is Kaige—we call him Super Nova—and his girlfriend, Nola." He pointed out the guy with dreads and the mocha-skinned woman who'd only formally agreed to join their enterprise earlier that morning. She sat in Kaige's lap and rested her head on his shoulder. A subtle smile curved her full lips upward. It was nice to see her happy and at ease in their group.

"Kaelyn DuChamp, you look familiar." Nova tilted his head and squinted a bit. "I think I'd remember a fancy name like that, though."

Nola smacked her guy on the chest. "It's a *lovely* name."

"Yeah, sounds like something I can't afford." He obviously was trying to compliment Kae.

"Please, ignore him. He doesn't mean anything bad by that." Nola grimaced.

"Well, anyway, she must look like someone else. You've never met her," Bryce jumped in, denying his friend's instinct. Before the intuitive man could insist, Carver returned. They didn't call him Meep for nothing. Not only did he drive a Roadrunner, but he was a fast fucker too. A trait that had come in handy when Roman had landed them in heaps of trouble as a teen.

"Thank you." Kaelyn sipped from the enormous water bottle.

"Go ahead and chug that. No need to be dainty with it. You must be dehydrated to have passed out like that." Bryce lifted the bottom of the container, forcing her to swallow more, faster. A dribble escaped her lips and trailed along her chin.

He snuffed a groan and wiped the drop with the pad of his thumb.

"If you're thirsty, drink up. Free refills." Roman surprised Bryce with his reassurance. Usually quiet, he seemed curious about their impromptu visitor.

"Yeah, we won't take your eagerness the wrong way. I like 'em big too." Carver grunted when the back of Bryce's hand smacked him in the gut.

"Not appropriate, asshole," Bryce growled.

"Since when do you expect us to have manners?" Holden chimed in. "We're mutts, not purebreds, remember?"

"I thought that was the way you liked things." Alanso raised a brow at Bryce. "Nothing refined, nothing classy… I think I get it now. You're in denial. You grew up with her?"

Kaelyn choked when Alanso pointed first at Bryce and then at her. She kept drinking through their banter until the entire bottle had been drained dry. Despite the blush creeping over her cheeks and across her décolletage, she held the vessel out to Meep. "Please?"

"Sure. Nothing to get embarrassed about. We appreciate a woman who can suck it down around here," Carver assured her, Hot Rods-style.

"Meep!" This time it was Nola who objected. "Next thing you'll be making 'that's what *he* said' jokes like the Powertools crew. Stop that!"

Good thing since Bryce had clenched his jaw and fisted his hands.

Sally came to the rescue. "It's habit, Kaelyn. Ignore them or feel free to rip them right back. That one is Carver, his roommate Roman and this guy here is Holden. Or Meep, Barracuda and Swinger, depending on who's talking. Sorry, we have these nicknames. It's a pain in the ass to get to know us. There are about a million of us and we each have at least two names... I don't know who thought that was a good idea."

Kaelyn laughed along with Sally. "As long as you give me a bit to remember them, it sounds fun to me."

"Maybe you need one too then. I have a few ideas." Swinger flashed his charming grin while Bryce gnashed his teeth. "Ours are based on our favorite cars. The ones we drive. And that was one hell of a ride I saw you two pull in with. Sexy. If you let us under your hood we could do a lot with that."

"So *anyway*, now that introductions have been made. Stupid formalities." Bryce grumbled. "Why the hell were you stranded on the side of the road in *my* town?"

"What are you, the mayor or something?" Kaelyn made him feel a hell of a lot better when she revealed some of her true inner core. He'd started to think maybe it had withered in their old stodgy environment. "Forget you. I had a flat tire. It's just bad luck that I also discovered your hiding place."

She glared at him, anger replacing the wounded, lost looks—not to mention the endless glances at his mouth—that had been crushing his heart.

Bryce wanted to set her straight, but he couldn't. She had the gist of it right. "You were running. Scared. I know myself that this town is on the path from Windsor. Especially if you're trying to keep off the interstates, avoiding being seen. For me it was a single tank of gas from home. And that's as far as you can go when you're broke. Lost. So who are you trying to escape, Kaelyn? Why?"

Tears filled her eyes. When he reached out she shook her head. "Don't touch me. I'm tired of liars thinking they can rule my life. You're just as bad as him."

"Who?" Rebel asked again.

"My father." She bit her trembling lower lip.

"Hey, whoever's got you frightened, don't worry. We won't let anyone bother you." Carver returned with more water and did what Bryce was banned from doing. He leaned down and hugged Kaelyn, offered her his strength and reassurance. That she accepted the gesture from a stranger over Bryce tore his guts out.

And earned his friend his undying appreciation.

He knew he could count on the Hot Rods. At least until Kaelyn blew his cover.

Revealed to them what a fake he really was.

"What did that jackoff do?" Bryce focused on what was most important—Kae.

"He tried to arrange a marriage for me. To sell me, essentially, to Montgomery Price, in exchange for the guy's support in the election and the boost to their images a grand wedding would provide." She sniffled. "I'm so stupid. I believed it was this whirlwind affair. That I'd finally found someone to replace...*you*. When I overheard my dad and Montgomery laughing at me, and my stupidity for not realizing the whole thing was fake, I called off the wedding. Daddy threatened to disown me."

Bryce cursed. He knew the weight a fortune could have when wielded against you. The finer things in life had always been more important to Kaelyn.

"So you took your platinum cards and ran," he finished for her. "He's probably already canceled them, lady."

"He did. And shut off service to my phone. It doesn't matter, though. I don't give a crap. I told him I don't want anything to do with him or his disgusting inheritance." She trailed off as tears spilled down her cheeks.

What? Though he'd unfettered himself from the same golden cuffs, he never would have imagined Kaelyn could make the same decision. Maybe the younger version of her wouldn't have. But this woman…

Bryce felt his respect for her burgeoning along with the bulge in his pants.

Chains disappearing into Holden's back pocket rattled as he took a clean handkerchief from his jeans and passed it to her. "Here, sweetheart."

She looked adorable and so out of place as she blew her nose into the skull-and-crossbones-dotted material. "Thanks."

"What do you mean, Kae? What did you do?" He couldn't believe she might be telling him what it sounded like. He wanted to hear her say it straight.

"I disowned *him* before he could do it to me. And that's when he grabbed me." She shivered and stared at her arm. "Like the snake he is. He struck fast, before I saw it coming. My own dad."

Only now did Bryce notice the ligature marks around her fine-boned wrists. That fucker. He'd laid his hands on her? He'd pay for that.

"They weren't going to let me leave." She trembled so hard her teeth chattered. Carver held on to her, encouraging her to finish in a low murmur. Promising her they would protect her. Rubbing circles on her narrow back.

Bryce had never loved the man as much as he did right then.

Because he sure as hell couldn't speak. And the fury in his eyes would terrify Kaelyn if she saw it unveiled.

"I bit him. When Montgomery tried to stop me next, I kneed him in the crotch like you showed me after Porsche Silverton told us her date had forced her into sex after the Valentine's Day dance." She sniffled but finished her story, patting Buster between his slumped ears when he whimpered, sensing her distress. "I ran and kept going until I got to your car. I've worn the key around my neck since you...left it behind. Like me. I drove it a lot, figuring it would tick you off if you knew. You never did let anyone touch your baby."

"Sounds like the Rebel I know," Swinger muttered.

Kaelyn shook her head as though she couldn't sort out the unfathomable realties that had shaped her new world. "I left with just what I had on me and in my purse. I drove as fast and far as I could until I hit a pothole in the road and blew out a tire."

She sobbed a few times before getting herself together.

"I couldn't even make it one day on my own." Then she did something that had him grinning despite their completely screwed-up situation—she cursed. "Motherfucker."

It sounded awkward...unused...as it flew from her mouth.

Eli chuckled, though the sound held as much tension as amusement. "Attagirl."

"Don't feel bad." Bryce sighed heavily, knowing he couldn't procrastinate another instant. "That's about what happened to me too. Except it wasn't only your dad. It was both of our fathers ganged up against me. They threatened to disinherit me—"

"Why?" She grew still as she looked up at him with those glittering eyes, diamond teardrops hanging off her lashes. Despite the pain, she licked her lips as she peered into his face. Subconsciously, he was sure.

He cleared his throat and glanced away.

"Don't worry about that. I told them they could shove their money. There was only one thing I needed to buy."

Kaige muttered a curse at Bryce's vagueness. He must have figured out where this was going.

"Don't give me that bull." Kaelyn climbed to her knees, getting in his face. "I was straightforward with you. Is it too much to ask for one jerk to do the same for me?"

She pounded on his collarbones, taking out her loss and desperation on him. He didn't mind.

And when she collapsed against his chest, crying, he didn't hesitate. His arms banded around her, cocooning her as best he could from the cruel world. Even though he knew his words would hurt her worse than the clutches that had left those stains on her wrist.

"Okay, lady. I swear I'll be honest with you from here on out. Always." He didn't give the oath lightly. "I'm sorry."

Whether he apologized to her or to the gang rallied around him, he wasn't sure. Both, he supposed.

"Just say it fast. Like a Band-Aid," Roman recommended.

"I didn't give a shit when they threatened me. With pictures of you and me camping out in your tree house. We always knew our families wouldn't approve of our...*friendship* since your dad and mine are political opponents. Anyway, you were fourteen, I was seventeen. They said I'd go to jail. They told me I'd molested you when I kissed you. And with us sharing that sleeping bag, snuggling, it looked pretty damning when your dad accused me of groping you—and other stuff— beneath the covers. They had evidence. And they were right. I did it. I knew I shouldn't have, but I couldn't help myself. You were too young and I made out with you anyway. Worse, I wished for more. Staying and keeping my hands off after that would have been impossible. I couldn't have denied that. No way would they stand for us crossing the lines they'd crafted between their parties, ruining the polarizing they'd done, pitting voters against each other over how different they were. We went against all that, bridged the gap. Still, I didn't give a shit when they held the pictures over my head. I checked it out on the Internet, figured I'd get in some trouble though maybe not as bad as they made it seem. But when I came back and told them to do their worst, they said they'd disown you...cut you off. Humiliate you so that no one we knew would accept you. Torture you with embarrassing proceedings and intrusive, public trials... I couldn't do it. Broke and cast out, I knew you would resent me. I couldn't do that to you.

"And let's face it. My dad had to have guessed I'd never follow his footsteps. I'd only have been a pain in his ass, smudging his image when I didn't color in the lines. This might have been the first time things got so fucked up between us, but it wouldn't have been the last. So I swore to leave quietly. To never come back. I told my dad to kill me for sympathy votes. So you wouldn't look for me. Honestly, they'd already destroyed me. What did it matter? Instead, they cooked up this story about me going to party in Europe, then they tried to buy me off to make it real and to make sure I didn't try to change my mind. I guess they thought I'd be content with fast cars, eager women and sitting around on a beach with my thumb up my ass. Fuck that. Like I'd take dirty money. I told them I'd build my own life. I'd only ever come back to make them miserable if they hurt you. I tried to protect you. I thought I was doing what was best. I'm sorry. I was immature and naive and... I'm sorry."

Bryce let go of Kaelyn. He swallowed the lump in his throat as he remembered the loss. The grief. Not for his old life. But for her.

He'd lived with it every single day. The thought of her happy and whole had been the only thing making it bearable. To find out it'd been for nothing...

All those years of agony.

All those years of lying by omission to his friends. Far more sordid in some ways, his past hadn't tortured him with the base suffering the rest of the guys had endured. He wasn't really one of them.

He might have pummeled the wall, put his fist through something, if Holden hadn't been there to lay his hand on Bryce's shoulder. To squeeze hard enough to remind him that his back was covered. But would it still be when they realized what this meant?

Rebel shot to his feet, making Buster bark and cower closer to Kaelyn. He turned to face his friends, hands spread wide as if to make a target of his chest for them. He deserved whatever they flung at him. "So now you know my deep, dark secret. I never wanted for a thing. I don't know what it's like to starve."

Bryce glanced at Roman, then away. "I've never been beat. Or abused...in other ways. I didn't have to watch my family suffer. I'm some twisted freeloader who took kindness that another, needier kid could have really used. Because I didn't know what else to do. Where else to go."

His breath sawed in and out of his lungs. His shame and ugliness finally out for them to judge as harshly as he deserved.

Except they didn't. Well, most of them.

"The way I see it, what you did took guts." Roman stepped in, bracing his hand on Rebel's shoulder. Sally seemed to be nodding, from what Bryce could tell out of the corner of his eye. Alanso too. "It wasn't any big deal for me to leave nothing for something better. I didn't have shit, so there wasn't anything to sacrifice."

Kaige hummed while hugging Nola to his chest. "That's true, Rebel."

"You're either the bravest or dumbest of us to forfeit a fortune for this." Holden chucked him in the arm.

Like that, Bryce deflated. They didn't hate him? Call him an imposter?

He wanted to laugh and cry at the same time. He'd hidden from them for so long, he felt naked in front of their assessing stares.

Until his gaze roamed to Carver. The man's maroon cheeks and clenched fists were as out of place on the usually easygoing guy as an amateur's wing and spinny rims would be on his Roadrunner.

"Meep—" He winced and prepared to be punched again, this time by someone who could knock out a tooth or three when his ex-friend cut him off.

"How fucking dare you?" Carver's hackles rose, making him seem much more intimidating than an average dude his size. "Guys like Barracuda suffered. Fucking day and night. Tortured by the conditions they were raised in. Hell, Roman still *does*. What about Kaige? He has nightmares about his dad killing his mom! I sucked nasty cocks for money to eat. Alanso and Cobra both lost their moms. Sally escaped a fucking *cult*. All the while you had a silver spoon in your fat face. You asshole poser, you never once knew what it was like. To be one of us."

"If I'm not worried, you shouldn't be." Barracuda put his hand on Carver's shoulder and squeezed. Or would have if his roommate hadn't shrugged him off, looking ready to spit.

"Fuck that." Meep lunged forward, damn that speedy fucker, getting in one solid blow straight to Bryce's gut. It didn't hurt nearly as much as the impact to Bryce's heart. Before Meep could rain more of his uncommon anger on Rebel, Roman snagged the back of his shirt. Kaige and Holden were a step behind, securing Carver's arms behind his back and escorting him to the kitchen.

"It's okay. I always knew I would be an outcast. Even among misfit mechanics." Bryce accepted Carver's rage, absorbed it though it stung like alcohol in an open wound. To his surprise, Kaelyn seemed to have his back.

"Oh my gosh." She ran her hands over his abs, making him groan. Not in pain. The adrenaline pumping through his system like high-octane gasoline magnified her simple touch. "Are you okay? I can't believe that man *hit* you."

He might have chuckled if his soul wasn't bruised. The tap hadn't injured him. Shit. They should have let Meep pound him and get it out of his system. With Kaelyn here, they'd lost their guaranteed method for blowing off steam.

How the hell could he fix this? He'd figure out a way. He had to.

In the meantime, Bryce accepted Kae's gentle tending as a consolation prize.

From the kitchen, Bryce heard Roman settling his best friend. Maybe later the guy would be capable of civility. Hopefully the grudge wouldn't last, though Bryce would understand if it did. Holden and Kaige rejoined the crowd in the living room, giving the roommates some space.

"I think we've had about enough." Eli sighed. Immediately his wife, Sally, rubbed lazy circles on his back. "You might not have suffered outright abuse like some of our Hot Rods, or poverty, or whatever other horrors some of us have. But there are a lot of ways to hurt a kid. Some of them not even anyone's fault."

Bryce thought of fate, which had stolen Cobra's mom. Sickness didn't discriminate.

"I believe we were brought together for a reason." Holden looked to each of them, deliberately pausing on Kaelyn, including her, before continuing. "Whatever family we had before doesn't matter. Hot Rods are thicker than blood."

Could he mean it?

"You're one of us, Rebel." Eli refused to blink as he promised. "Don't ever doubt that. However you got here is irrelevant. Carver will come around."

More cursing echoed from the kitchen, though somewhat less heated than before.

Roman hauled his roommate down the hall. A door slammed seconds later.

"You had a good reason to do what you did." Alanso peered at Kaelyn, who stood tall beside Bryce. At least until she bent and scooped up Buster, who kept growling and barking while facing the hallway, where Carver had disappeared.

Rebel swallowed hard and thought of the threats his biological parent had made. Things that would have irreparably injured the one person he gave a fuck about. The same girl who circled around in front of him now, trembling lip and huge, watering eyes making his arms ache to hold her.

Except she was awfully grown up these days.

And looking like the fine lady she'd been destined to become. Could she have been meant to be his from the start? How else could you explain her landing on his doorstep right when he was settled enough to claim her.

Only one way to find out, he supposed.

Especially since she peeked up at his mouth, even now.

Bryce took one stride toward Kaelyn, closing the gap between them. He didn't force her to accept him, not after what she'd confessed. But he held out his arms, wide open. The hunger in his eyes had to be apparent because he'd never wanted something as badly as her.

She stepped into the circle of his embrace. And that's all the permission he needed.

He slammed his mouth over hers, tasting the salt of her pain and the honey of her innocence combined. He caressed her lips with his, trying to take some of her hurt and easing his own with her sweetness.

The chemistry that had shocked him that long-ago summer, once he'd been old enough to give the connection a name, came roaring back to life like a five-hundred-horsepower street stroker engine. They grappled with each other, Kae practically climbing him as she attempted to get closer. The strangled whimpers she fed him had Buster pawing at them, dissolving the moment.

Although they broke apart reluctantly, some hope filled the darkest places in his soul.

From the tremulous smile she rewarded him with, he guessed the same was true for her.

She touched her fingertips to her swollen lips.

"Well then." Sally spoke softly as she approached. "Why don't you come with me and take some time to get yourself together, Kaelyn? I think we could use a few minutes to process this. And I think Bryce better go speak to Tom. That's Eli's dad. He's kind of our adopted dad too. Anyway, I have a stash of these cool bath bombs that Nola bought me for my birthday. They're pretty relaxing. Smell nice and make your skin soft too..."

Damn her, Mustang was right. Bryce had made things right, finally, with his garagemates. Or at least he'd tried. He could work on Carver later. But Tom deserved to know the truth. To hear it from him directly. A hell of a lot too late. Hopefully, better that than never.

"If you really don't mind, I'd love to get cleaned up. A soak sounds wonderful. Along with some space…to think." Kaelyn lifted her chin as if their kiss hadn't shaken her to the bones, as it had him. It was impossible to hide the dilation of her gorgeous cerulean eyes or the pounding of her pulse in her fine neck or the fullness of her swollen, reddened lips when she licked another taste of him from her own skin, though. "Thank you."

"You're welcome." Bryce couldn't help the insinuation in his tone.

Holden snorted, while Kaige laughed and bounced Nola on his lap, where she perched once more.

"Careful, Rebel. If you want to do that again, you shouldn't rev the engine too high and risk blowing a gasket. Or, you know, scaring her off," Swinger warned his friend. Though his eyes held a hint of humor, truth underlined the advice.

Kaelyn set them straight. "I don't panic easily. Not anymore. And definitely not because of *him*."

She folded her hands in front of her, a gesture straight out of finishing school. A tell she'd always had. Or at least since Bryce had taught her to play poker in their tree house. A forbidden pastime her aristocratic grooming would never have approved for a young lady.

"Who's lying now?" He couldn't say what drove him to call her on it. Unless it was the susceptibility she'd seeded in him. Misery loved company.

She surprised him again by flipping him off. The combination of her ladylike suit, though wrinkled, and the crass gesture had him hard—*harder*—in a second. He chuckled as she stormed off with Sally, who offered to lend her some additional girly crap and help her get settled.

Kaelyn DuChamp terrified him. She made him want things he couldn't have. Not if he cared about doing what was in her best interest, like he had when she was younger.

And that, he believed, was the definition of love.

Fuck.

CHAPTER THREE

Bryce plodded up the stairs to Tom's house, which perched across the driveway from the Hot Rods' garage and their massive apartments above the commercial space. His fist hovered a few inches from the front door as he gathered his courage and rehearsed his confession.

It would kill him to disappoint the man inside.

Without having to knock, the door opened and Tom jerked his chin toward the kitchen. "I figured you'd be stopping by. Everyone was acting funny when I asked where you'd gone. They must think I'm senile or some crap. You kids were never good at sneaking around when you were hooligan teens and you're no better now. What the hell is going on?"

Despite the weights crushing his heart, Rebel cracked a grin. They'd always thought they were so slick, until Tom busted them...or let them get away with minor infractions.

He'd known exactly the right balance to strike with the gang of stray juveniles he'd taken in.

"What's so funny?" Tom swatted Rebel in the back of the head then shoved him toward the kitchen table, where so many of the Hot Rods' troubles were hashed out.

"Nothing. Nothing." Bryce held his hands up. "Seriously. I think that's a nervous tic or something."

Honestly, he couldn't help smiling.

Despite the gravity of the situation, a sliver of Bryce celebrated having Kaelyn in his life again for however long he might manage it. That kiss had been everything he'd dreamed of as a teen, and beyond.

"It's not like you to be edgy." Tom narrowed his eyes as he took a seat across the scarred wood from Bryce, who still stood. "Usually you leave that to Roman. So why don't you spit it out? Tell me quick how you've fucked up."

"Why assume I screwed up?"

"Would you be here pussy-footing around if you hadn't?" Tom grunted. "These little chats are becoming a regular thing lately. Eli, Al, Sally, Kaige...now you. Think I could have my own talk show on TV? No? Fine. So let's put it on the table and figure out how to fix it."

The reassurance that it *could* be handled settled Bryce.

He took a deep breath, leaned forward and held onto the edge of the table. "I lied to you."

"About what?" Tom didn't seem angry, more curious.

"Pretty much everything. Where I came from. My...*situation*." Rebel cleared his throat.

"Bryce, you'd have had to tell me something in order for it to be a lie." A wave of Tom's hand flashed knuckles that seemed more gnarled than Rebel remembered.

"I guess I was embarrassed to admit the truth. Afraid you'd take me back if you knew I didn't have it as bad as the rest of the Hot Rods." He hung his head.

"You mean because your dad is some highfalutin senator? A rich bastard?" Tom crossed his arms. "Huh. Didn't make him any less of an asshole, did it? He certainly didn't deserve you or any other kid."

"You knew? All along?" Rebel sat down hard, letting the air rush out of his lungs. "And you didn't send me away?"

"Rebel, you're the only kid who's ever shown up at the youth shelter in custom-tailored navy slacks and a blazer. Your story about the store feeling bad for you and donating them was lame. And so was your poker face." Tom laughed as if remembering that day as clearly as Bryce did. "We did have the Internet, even back then. It wasn't hard to pin you down when you only came from two states away. Especially when your father was using your so-called charity work in Europe to pander for votes. Sorry, Rebel."

"You're not telling me anything I don't know." He shrugged.

"Look, there's no way in hell I'd ever have let him have you after using you like that. There'd be no one to watch out for you since your mom had left you in that snake pit alone. I shouldn't judge, though—maybe she didn't have a choice. He might have threatened to harm her, or you, if she'd stayed."

"What do you mean?" Bryce leaned forward, his head tipping. He couldn't hardly remember his mother. Not as more than a warm, soft memory comprised of big smiles and bigger hugs.

"Oh, uh..." Tom cleared his throat. "I guess it's time we both came clean. After you became one of the family, I hired an investigator. I stockpiled as much evidence as I could collect, the only kind of insurance I knew how to get. In case your dad tried to reverse his banishment—when it became convenient for advancing his agenda. The PI asked a lot of questions. Interviewed your old housekeepers, stuff like that. I'm sorry, Rebel, but I think your dad chased your mom out too. All accounts say she was unhappy once she realized your father had never loved her, only wanting an heir and a spot in her father's party. She threatened to leave your dad and take you with her. If your grandfather hadn't had a massive stroke a few weeks later, she probably would have gotten you both out."

Bryce's heart sank as he realized his mother probably hadn't died, like he'd always been told. Like Kaelyn, he'd taken too much at face value. Then a ray of hope burst inside him. "Did my father lie about her? Do you think she's still out there somewhere? Could I track her down?"

"No. Sorry, son." Tom grimaced. "She really did get pneumonia. Probably a few months later than you thought, though. She didn't last the winter without a place to stay. Her coward friends were afraid to cross your dad, I think. And, like you, she refused to take a penny of his dirty money. At least that's what it seemed like from what scraps we could pry out of people. Certainly her bank account ran dry the day after she took off. I can't tell you how badly I wish the shelter had been open back then and that she'd found her way there. Like you did."

Bryce recalled hounding his father about where his mom had gone. How he was told over and over that a boy couldn't understand adult business. To accept that she wasn't coming back. And finally when his father had "cracked" nearly half a year later and spilled the secret that his wife had passed away.

Had the single tear that had tracked down Raymond Ellington's—Bryce refused to ever consider that scum his father—cheek been real?

Likely it had been. Except borne of relief rather than grief.

"I was such a fucking moron." Bryce had the urge to smack himself in the forehead, though he knew nothing could obliterate the shock and the dull ache blossoming in his chest.

"Nah, you were a kid."

"What about Peter DuChamp? Have any dirt on him?" Bryce didn't care so much about himself at the moment. He'd spent years missing his mother. Knowing the truth hurt, but it couldn't bring her back. They needed to help Kaelyn break free of the same glass prison that had ensnared him and his mom.

Their fathers wouldn't win this time.

"No, but we can find some if we need it. Why?" Tom sat back and steepled his fingers over surprisingly toned abs. For an older guy, he could still kick some ass.

"His daughter, Kaelyn... She's here. And she needs our help breaking away.

Permanently. Her father tried to force her into marrying some dirtwad politician. Maybe a new running mate for her dad. He's my dad's rival, you know?"

"Yeah. I never cared much for politics, but I've kept my eyes open when I heard about those two duking it out. Anything to do with your father, really. Maybe we could set them against each other somehow?" Tom sighed. "Let me think on it tonight. I can make contact with those old informants, see what we turn up."

"Jesus." Bryce rubbed his temples. "It's the same pattern over and over, isn't it? Using people, threatening them, twisting the power bought by cash into a weapon that bludgeons people into submission. I thought I was so smart, getting out of the game. I can't believe I didn't think about how Kaelyn would be their pawn too eventually. I imagined her thriving there. A protected princess. A material girl put up on a shelf like a trophy and worshiped like the rest of the fine things they collected. Not being used like they tried to do to me. I didn't belong there, but she always seemed like she did."

"You were young. And doing your best to survive." Tom growled. "*I* should have asked you about it long ago, realized there might be more kids who needed help. That one's on me.

You were immature. I was the adult. You know, I always thought you were mourning your mom. I didn't realize you'd left someone else behind."

"It nearly killed me, Tom." To finally be able to say it out loud had Bryce's heart cracking. "I only did it because I thought I was keeping her safe. That's all that mattered to me. She was scared today. Hurt. Angry. I failed her."

"We both did. But I'll make it up to your girl, I promise. We'll get her out of this mess now. Find a way to keep her father, and yours, from interfering in your lives ever again. You know they're coming, don't you, Bryce? They're not going to let this go. Not with a loose end out there that could hurt their campaigns. It's an election year."

"I know." He rubbed his temple, already preparing himself for the fight ahead. "I hope we have enough time to show Kae this could be her place too, or help her find her own path. She's not going to trust me easily, Tom."

"You might be surprised." He grinned. "I can't wait to meet her myself and see what I can feel out. Maybe I'll give Ms. Brown a call and get her take on the situation. Nola's mom is a great sounding board. And you know she'll keep her lips zipped. Plus she's way better at using the computer than I am.

Between the two of us, and you kids, I'm pretty sure we can come up with a plan."

"Son of a bitch, what did I get myself into?" Bryce couldn't help but laugh. With the meddling that was surely about to start, he stood no chance at resisting the chemistry that still zinged between him and Kae. Not that he wanted to.

"Rebel, can I give you some unsolicited advice?" Tom paused as though he'd really hold his tongue if Bryce didn't give him the go-ahead.

"Of course." He'd never ignore his adopted dad's wisdom.

"Be careful not to let your girl think your hatred of the corruption that scarred you includes everything from that life. If you're not cautious, she might assume your crappy attitude is aimed at her and the pampering she had while you roughed it." Tom laughed and waved him off when he tried to explain how he'd had everything he needed and then some with the Londons. "You're going to be in for it. Kaelyn probably doesn't even realize how spoiled she's been."

"Maybe I wish I could keep her that way." Bryce sighed. "I can't give her everything she's used to, but I can try my best to make things easy for her."

"Who says that's what she wants?" Tom asked as he slapped Bryce on the back. "Why don't you ask her how she sees her future? Help her figure it out. So much has changed, she's got to be confused. And lost. Show her there's another way. And that she's welcome to drive down that road with you."

"How do you know that's what *I* want?" Bryce didn't outright deny it.

"Because I know you. I can see the hope you're trying to bury. Don't give up without a fight, Bryce. Maybe you can have it all. Why not try?" For a moment, a cloud crossed Tom's face. "Not everyone gets a second chance. Don't blow yours."

"I won't." Bryce owed it to the man, who'd lost the love of his life too soon. "I promise. Thank you, Tom. *Dad*."

They hugged, quick though fierce. Then he strode for the door before the mist in his eyes could condense into tears.

By the time Bryce crossed to the apartment, he'd gotten himself mostly under control. He loitered in the hallway with Holden, Kaige and a couple of the guys. They seemed to understand how much he needed them nearby to reassure him of the strength of their link. For the most part, finding out about his past hadn't changed what they thought of the person they'd come to love over the last decade. They made that clear by teasing him about his *girlfriend* and otherwise making jabs like they would any other day.

They didn't even judge him when he laid his palm on the bathroom door, around the corner from his own room, knowing Kaelyn was in there. So close, and yet untouchable.

They also didn't try to stop him from kicking it in when she shrieked loud and shrill enough to shatter the mirror. Or at least it seemed like she had.

Had she fainted again? Hit her head? Was she okay?

He didn't wait to find out.

***

Kaelyn glanced around the bathroom. Simple yet functional, it seemed spartan compared to the opulence she'd lived with her whole life, long enough not to notice the fine materials or elegant fixtures until they'd been replaced with basic porcelain, cracked in a few spots. What she hadn't been as oblivious to was the hole in her existence Bryce had left when he'd disappeared. Or the wounds his father had caused, like water damage seeping through the cracks opened by her insecurity and eroding the glue that had bonded her and Bryce. The man had used every opportunity to brag about his son's conquests in Europe. And she'd taken the bait. Hook, line and sinker.

She felt like one of the broken tiles she spotted on the shower surround. A less than perfect version of her old self.

No matter how pissed off she wanted to be, she couldn't help but be sad instead. Obviously, their friendship hadn't meant the same thing to him as it had to her. Stupidly, she'd even dreamed that someday they might have...more. Once he'd gotten over his foolish sense of nobility, given their age difference. What was a few years' gap once they were no longer teenagers?

She'd never had the chance to find out.

Then again, how could she blame him for doing the same thing she had by fleeing? Especially if, in some convoluted way, he'd thought his absence would insulate her from her dad's scheming.

It had, for a while.

Hating Bryce became impossible when she thought with her head, instead of her heart. *Darn it.*

Every part of her ached. At least she could do something about the muscles that had knotted with tension as she listened to the bitter truths Bryce spewed to his friends and to her. She trailed her fingers through the steamy water filling the plastic tub.

A knock on the door startled her.

"Kaelyn?" one of the Hot Rods' women called to her.

"Yes?" She clutched the borrowed robe around her, amazed by how soft it was despite the plain-ish synthetic material.

"Feel free to raid Nola's stash of bath bombs and goop in the baskets on the surround," Sally offered, then begrudgingly admitted, "as much as I hate to say it, they do feel nice and help a girl relax."

"Ah, thank you." Kae didn't think they'd understand what her usual spa regime entailed. With no plans to enlighten them about the benefits of organic Japanese seaweed, she surrendered the terrycloth hugging her and dipped her toe in the bath. When had she become such a snob?

Her father had counted on that weakness to keep her captive.

Regardless of the blows she'd been dealt in the past several hours, her determination had not shaken. She would build her own life. One she could maintain and enjoy. The finer things hadn't guaranteed her happiness.

A sigh escaped her lips as warm water flowed around her, surrounding her in heat that penetrated her weary bones. For a while, she rested her head on the molded off-white tub and allowed her mind to drift, blissfully blank.

When the temperature dropped a bit, she drained some water, then refilled it with a fresh batch. Tendrils of steam curled around her.

"Doing okay in there?" Nola this time.

Kaelyn wondered if none of them took marathon soaking sessions. Probably they had to work for a living. If the size of the operation below was any indication, they had enough jobs to keep them busy for a century. Screw it. She didn't feel like hurrying. Or facing Bryce again.

"Great," she called softly. Maybe if she kept saying it, it would be true.

"Let me know if you need anything." The other woman chuckled. "I don't mind bringing you a glass of wine. Or, you know, a whole bottle. Whatever it takes."

"Thank you." Kaelyn giggled for the first time since she'd realized her father had tried to arrange her marriage in some medieval feudal proposition that would bind her and his backers permanently. "I think I'll try one of these giant bath-salt things."

"Go ahead." Nola sounded like she might be smiling. "Take your time."

Kaelyn poked around in the brightly colored blobs of baking soda and fruity-smelling oil. She sniffed one. *Mmm, mango.* Then she nudged a couple aside to dig for a flash of silver that caught her eye. A star. It reminded her of the nights she and Bryce had snuck outside to their tree house. Okay, more like a tree castle, to stare at the twinkling lights high above their heads.

She recalled a night when she'd forgotten her sweater. After curling up against the furnace of his chest while they sat and talked for hours, she'd been careful never to bring a jacket again. The weight of his arm around her shoulders—casual and friendly—had been a highlight of those evenings. He'd felt like her rock when she'd rested her head against him. For a moment, when he'd kissed her, she'd wanted to believe he could be that support again.

Better yet, maybe she could be his too this time.

The horror, and acceptance, on his face when his friend had rejected him had riled every instinct she possessed. Comforting had been second nature.

It'd always been like that between them.

When she'd disappointed her father by tripping on her ridiculous gown and falling down the stairs in front of guests at a campaign kickoff, he'd held her as she cried. Then he'd transformed her tears into laughter despite her sprained ankle.

When he'd pissed his father off by hanging out with their maid's son, she was the only person he'd told the real reason that Marietta had been fired. Together they'd arranged for Kaelyn to slip her cash to help out afterward.

They'd made an awesome team.

Why couldn't things have turned out like she'd imagined back then? Probably because there was too much she hadn't understood. Still didn't. Maybe she'd never known him at all.

Kaelyn held the starry bath bar in front of her, admiring the shine as she considered making a wish. It must have held more moisturizing oils than she realized because it slipped through her fingers, like a lot of other things in her life. With a distinct plop, it crashed into the bath and fizzed more vehemently than she anticipated.

In fact, the froth that started out white turned blue as it bubbled near the lip of the tub. The water morphed, changing colors that might have been pretty if she hadn't been worried about staining her hosts' bathmat, or the entire tile floor, if the thing went bananas.

When she lifted her arm from the mushrooming foam, she realized that oodles of the glitter that had coated the bath bomb now stuck to her skin like the flambéed bananas foster gone wrong she'd witnessed in an exclusive restaurant once.

"Oh. Oh, no." She stood up and realized the sparkles had turned her into some cross between the Tin Man and that horrible rhinestone-encrusted dress Mrs. Black had worn to her father's last charity ball. "Holy crap."

Soft knocking came at the door, except she was too embroiled in the battle against the bling to respond quickly, or at all.

Another knock.

Kaelyn began to thrash in the tub, trying to knock some of the glitter off and disperse the foam that rose like a skyscraper on top of the water's surface. It would topple any second. She dove for the drain, knocking it out but grunting and shouting—something she almost never did, it wasn't ladylike—in the process.

Just as she lost the war, two things happened simultaneously. A wave of gleaming foam splashed onto the floor and deposited some of the sticky shimmer while the door burst open and banged against the poor black-painted vanity, which certainly didn't deserve such abuse.

"What the hell—?" Bryce shot into the room, skidding on the blob near the tub before he could stop.

Kaelyn shrieked and covered herself, or as many of the important bits as she could manage with two handfuls of twinkling bubbles. Great.

Hot on Bryce's heels, the rest of his roommates swarmed the bathroom as if prepared to fight off ninjas that had rappelled through the window. Shocked and embarrassed to have sullied their bathroom, Kaelyn could only stand and stare at her audience as Bryce struggled to regain his footing.

Nola rushed to her aid. "Guys, this isn't some kind of peep show. Jeez. Leave her alone. Nobody's dying in here. Stand down."

Just as Nola reached toward the towel rack, Buster McHightops flew in from the hallway, barking his fool puppy head off at the sight of the mountain of gleaming froth. He nipped at a wayward pile of suds, oblivious that he'd cut Nola off.

She shooed him toward the hall, stopping short and skidding on a slick patch of tile in the process. Her eyes grew wide and she braced herself for the inevitable crash.

Before she could fall, Kaige rushed in and swooped her up.

"Careful, babe." He seemed more upset than was warranted as he dropped to his knees and hugged her tight. "It's not just you we've got to worry about now."

A hush fell over the room, which was entirely too small for the gang now packing the tiny space. Nola peeked over her boyfriend's shoulder at the bug-eyed stares of their partners. If there'd been any way to sneak past undetected from her post at the center of the bubblestorm, Kaelyn would have slunk away. Instead she hunkered down in the tub, using the lingering foam as cover, though it had started to fizzle away bit by bit.

The air in the room was charged in an instant.

"Did that come out funny, or did you mean it like it sounded?" Eli—the guy they called King Cobra—tipped his head and studied the pair huddled together on the bathmat. Blond dreads and blue eyes made Kaige striking, but the pure adoration in his gaze as he looked at the woman he cradled melted Kaelyn's heart.

Nola cupped Kaige's cheeks in her palms and kissed the tip of his nose then nodded briefly.

"We were going to wait a little bit. Until the doctor has a chance to give us the thumbs-up. There are tests and stuff. To make sure everything is normal." Kaige's voice sounded gruff and thick. "But, yeah. Nola's pregnant. We're going to have a baby. A mini Hot Rod."

Mustang Sally shrieked and skidded across the floor to kneel beside the couple. She encompassed them both in a bear hug. "That's fantastic."

"Are you sure?" Nola swallowed hard, though she didn't look away from Sally. "I was a kind of afraid…"

"Of what?" Alanso said something in rapid-fire Spanish that no one seemed to understand. "Don't say something to piss me off on such a happy day either."

"Well." Nola shrugged. "It's so new. You know. Stuff."

No one looked at Kaelyn, but she felt bizarrely out of place. She tried to read between the lines of their sketchy conversation and failed miserably.

"And we all live here. How will a baby fit in? Will it cramp your style?" She swallowed hard. "Plus, I didn't want anyone to think I did it on purpose. To trap Kaige into staying with me or something crazy. It was the night of your wedding, Eli. Kaige forgot to wear a condom that one time. It was a mistake. A happy one. I mean it wasn't intentional, but I wouldn't change it either."

Kaelyn almost broke her silence at the woman's pure nervousness. Even she could tell Nola's concerns were unfounded. Her friends adored her. They would never think something so despicable about her. What would it be like to have that kind of unflinching support? She shivered, wishing she knew.

"Stop being ridiculous." Alanso spat some more Spanish words that had to have been curses.

"Nola, I get what you're saying." Holden laid a hand on her shoulder. It seemed more reassuring than a brotherly touch. "But Al's right. Don't go any further. There's no need to worry. We love you. You're part of us now. And it's no surprise using protection slipped your minds that night. We were all th—"

This time Roman did glance at Kaelyn. Right before he smacked Holden in the gut, cutting him off by stealing his air.

Carver covered, coming to the rescue of the stony-faced man they called Barracuda. Apparently, they'd worked out some of their tension since she'd seen them last. Funny that the harder of the two had been more forgiving. If she'd met Roman on the street, without Bryce's endorsement, she might have been frightened of him. Lost eyes, deep lines on his face and tattoos that spoke of a life full of tough living—skulls, flames, dice, booze and drugs. He intimidated her. Enough that she nearly forgot about what it sounded like Holden had been about to say.

"Does Tom know?" Bryce changed the subject, smoothing things over like he always had. It was hard to imagine him as the rebel his friends called him when she saw him as a peacekeeper. "He's gonna freak out. In a good way, I mean."

"I hope you understand." Nola bit her lip. "I asked him for advice. I think my mom might have let it slip anyway, now that they're besties."

"Hell, Cobra, your old man knew before *I* did." Kaige rolled his eyes, then met Eli's stare before glancing back to the woman he held so close to his heart. "Who doesn't lean on Tom in a crisis, babe? We understand."

"And you have nothing to worry about." Sally kissed her friend on the cheek. "We're excited for you. *Thrilled*. I can't wait to be part of this baby's life. If you'll let me. Us."

"Of course." Nola blinked furiously as her eyes filled with moisture. "I wouldn't want to raise a kid in any other family."

She clutched Kaige's hand, her rich skin turning white at the knuckles. Had she worried they'd ostracize her? Kaelyn had only known them a matter of hours and she could have guaranteed that wouldn't be the case. She'd never met a more tightly bonded pack of people.

Loneliness swamped her.

She had to get out of there. Somewhere private, where she didn't have to face how utterly solitary she was compared to this network of comrades that included her one-time best friend.

Envy didn't look good on her.

"You guys?" Kaelyn hated to interrupt. Still, she couldn't even wipe the tears streaming down her cheeks since her hands were attempting to grant her an iota of modesty. "That's super touching, but can someone hand me a towel or the robe or...*something*?"

As her skin cooled, her nipples began to harden. At least she told herself it was the environment and not the guy she'd had a crush on as a teenager that did the trick. Seeing him like this, relaxed and surrounded by genuine, caring friends, she couldn't help but be jealous. No wonder he'd never come back for her.

"Shit. Sorry." Bryce lunged for the robe then crossed to her.

Not before his garagemates stole a few more glances, though.

"Don't be so quick to cover up, honey. It's a nice view. Though I'm not sure if you look more like a super classy stripper or one of those sparkly vampires with all that glitter going on." Carver cracked up as he leaned his hip against the sink and openly admired her. She knew some of his brashness was really aimed at mashing Bryce's buttons, so she didn't hold it against him. Besides, it was nice to know they found her attractive despite the two sexy women in their midst. "Either way, you're doing 'em proud."

"I'm going to kick your ass." Bryce swiped at his friend, but the other guy ducked.

"What? I said *classy* stripper!" Meep snorted as he made a break for it, evading capture while shoving through the crowd of his friends, dispersing some of them into the hallway. The crowd thinned.

"Rough-housing in the bathroom is a good way for one of you to end up in the emergency room with an absurd story again." Sally peeked around the crowd huddled in the bathroom. "Quit that before you knock into Nola. Besides, if you don't give Kaelyn some privacy, she'll think we're total pervs."

Holden choked, though Kaelyn couldn't quite understand why.

"We are," Roman muttered, earning a glare from Bryce. He held his hands up and out. "Okay, okay. Leaving. Glad to see you're not drowning yourself in our tub or some such, Kaelyn."

He stopped short of rolling his eyes at Bryce's overprotective urges, though it seemed as if it took some effort.

Surprisingly quick for a herd of built mechanics and a pair of women, they filed out, leaving her alone with Bryce.

And very naked.

CHAPTER FOUR

The shutting door unleashed a report at least as jarring as that of a rifle shot. Kaelyn should know, since an elaborate skeet shooting range occupied a section of the basement of her family's mansion. The powerful sound had nothing on the intensity of Bryce's stare, though, as he scanned her from head to toe.

Chills raced through her body, shaking her. Although she was feeling the effect of the cooling water that still dripped off her skin, she knew her body's reaction had a heck of a lot more to do with the guy stalking toward her than it did with the temperature of her bathwater.

"You're cold," he murmured as he approached. Was he daring her to call him a liar? To admit that she'd never been as sizzling inside as when he looked at her...like *that*?

Knowing that the horror stories of his endless string of beauties were false, she gave herself permission to feel all the things she'd buried. Overwhelming attraction swamped her. She could let him take care of her. He would. In many ways.

Kaelyn didn't nod or shake her head, but instead continued to meet his gaze despite the urge to turn away or blink. Anything to sever this unnatural connection they'd always shared. After having it stolen once, she couldn't bring herself to give it up, even if indulging herself was supremely foolish.

So she took the time to admire the changes in this man she'd once known so well. Maybe better than herself. Shirtless, the ink that accentuated his defined muscles mesmerized her as did his new, rugged frame. Inside, she could still see the things she'd loved most about him—the kindness in his soft gray eyes, the thoughtfulness he displayed as he plucked a towel from the bar on the wall, out of her reach.

"I hope you don't mind. It's mine." He grimaced. "I would get you a clean one out of the closet, but I think it's Holden's turn on laundry duty and he sucks at it. Puts it off until there's hardly anything left."

"This is fine." Despite what he might think of her, she wasn't stuck-up. Or at least not on purpose. She'd always had things handled for her. Towels laundered and folded by the house staff, replaced after each shower or bath before she bothered to think about how they never disappeared for long. This one smelled much nicer. Like his soap instead of some floral detergent.

Their fingers brushed when she tried to accept the cotton from his broad, calloused hands. The dings and nicks in his knuckles, and the occasional shadows beneath his nails, made her aware of the hard work he put in each day. At Hot Rods. A place he clearly loved.

Another shiver ran through her at their fleeting connection. Or maybe at the knowledge that he had found his bliss. She bit her lip to keep it from trembling, but he noticed the tears burning her eyes anyway.

"Shit. I'm sorry about the rest of the gang. They didn't mean to embarrass you. We're not big on personal boundaries." He cleared his throat at that.

Kaelyn shushed him and stood still as he knocked foam from her body, then bundled her in his well-worn towel. Between the scent of him—pure, masculine, clean, evergreen— and the softness he pressed to her flesh with those deft, if mammoth, fingers, she trembled yet again.

When he swaddled her in his arms and smothered her in the heat of his body, she quit attempting to resist. Instead, she rested her head on his shoulder and allowed him to care for her as he lifted her from the tub and set her on a fuzzy bathmat that had barely avoided being gilded by the extra-sparkly froth. The cartoon car-shaped rug felt divine when she curled her toes into it.

For the first time in a while she felt...safe.

Like the disaster her life had become might not be so scary after all. It might be nothing like what she'd planned for herself, but these people she'd stumbled across had rallied around Bryce. She'd bet none of them had a straightforward journey to this refuge where they'd grown to accept and cherish their differences.

The concern they'd shown for Bryce made her certain they would never give up on each other. And if she could pretend, for a few fleeting ticks of the clock, that their protective bubble included her, why shouldn't she?

Especially if Bryce was willing to keep holding her and rocking her and murmuring things as he glided his hand and the towel across her skin.

"You smell so good." The truth slipped out of Kaelyn as he returned the relaxation she'd gleaned from the steamy water.

"I could say the same." Husk infiltrated Bryce's timbre, roughening his voice, though not his touch. He knelt then nuzzled her belly as he began drying her thighs. "Honey, you might as well move your hands so I can do a good job here. I've pretty much seen it all anyway."

Kaelyn balked. "Maybe on your other women, but not me."

She couldn't help her old beliefs from slipping out.

"Do you mean Nola and Sally?" Bryce paused at her acerbic tone.

"Sorry, sorry." She swallowed hard and shook her head. "I wouldn't say something like that about your friends' ladies. It's just that your dad…"

"What?" He gritted his teeth. "What did that fucker do?"

"After you left, he seemed chattier. He'd always find me to tell me how proud he was that you were *seeing* some beautiful woman or other in Europe." She couldn't help the bitterness draining from her. "He would tell me how charming they were, how worldly, how—"

"I get the picture." Bryce gripped her tighter than he probably intended. "Listen. I hooked up with women. I'm not saying I was some kind of monk. But they weren't that frequent and I certainly didn't have any meaningful relationships. I haven't since…"

He swallowed hard, then looked directly into her eyes.

"No one's meant to me what you did. Do," he promised. Except something flickered in his gaze when he rubbed the back of his neck.

Suddenly, she didn't want to know. For the first time in forever, part of her blossomed, yearning to be touched. It'd been ages since she felt compelled to explore. "Hey, you don't need to explain. It's not like I'm a virgin either."

He winced at that.

Some selfish part of her kept her from telling him how bland her experiences had been. How boring. Unfulfilling.

"Besides, Kae, it wouldn't matter if I'd slept with a thousand women. None could compare to you." Bryce melted her last shreds of resistance. "Who are you going to trust—my father or me?"

She touched his cheek, hoping he could tell she felt the same about him. Between him and the evil bastard who'd raised him, there was no contest. Bryce deserved her faith. At least she prayed he did.

"So I'll be honest. If you think I really had my eyes closed those times we went skinny dipping..." He caught himself, maybe because he noticed her eyes narrowing as she thought yet again of how naïve she'd been.

Unfortunately it was true. And her chill returned.

"Fuck, Kae." He growled. "I can't think when you're around. That was dumb. I'm sorry. And I was a jerk for sneaking a peek back then."

"You're not *really* sorry, are you?" The revelation awed her. She'd tempted him? Those times he'd seemed oblivious to her crush—could he have actually felt something?

"Ah. Honestly?" He blew out a sigh that fluttered his hair over his creased brow.

Her fingers curled into fists to avoid burying themselves in the strands. Still, she nodded as she looked him straight in the eye. So she saw it, when he told the pure, unadulterated truth.

"No. I'm not. They're some of my favorite memories. You were gorgeous." His pupils dilated as his praise gave her the courage to let go of some of her insecurities and her death grip on her goods.

His Adam's apple bobbed after she bared her breasts to his stare. When he rocked forward slightly, she wondered if he really meant to lick his lips right then. Distracted by his intense admiration, her hand between her legs fell away also.

"Fuck me." He moaned. "You *are* gorgeous, I meant. More than I ever dreamed, Kaelyn.

Lush. Filled out from that girl's body. You're the most beautiful woman I've ever seen."

Squirming, she shifted restlessly before him.

"I'm making you uncomfortable." He squeezed his eyes closed, causing wrinkles where she'd never seen them on his youthful countenance. "I'm screwing this up."

"You're not." She reached out and cupped his handsome face, enjoying the rasp of his light beard on her palms. "I thought you didn't feel it. I mean, you never acted like we were more than friends. Would ever be. So when your dad told me...I believed."

A lump formed in her throat and she swallowed. Hard.

"Ah, Kae." Bryce lunged to his feet, enfolding her in the towel and lifting her as though she weighed no more than Buster McHightops. He pivoted, placing her on the sink so he could meet her gaze once again. The towel rested beneath her, ensuring the cool surface of the counter didn't reach her, the same way he insulated her from reality.

Maybe that was why she didn't flinch when he put his hands on her knees and pressed them apart, insinuating his bulk between them. Though his broad chest tapered to a trim waist, she spread her thighs for him, making it all too easy to imagine what it might be like to be intimate with him.

As opposed to the gentlemen she'd taken before, he'd be raw and exciting. He'd strip away propriety and leave wildness behind. What kind of etiquette was there for exposing yourself so completely? Body and soul.

She didn't know.

But she hoped he'd teach her.

Kaelyn reached around Bryce's bare chest to splay her hands on his back. Even spreading her fingers apart as far as possible, she didn't feel as though she held much of him. He was so big. As if he'd grown larger than life since she'd seen him last.

"It feels good to have you hug me again, Kae," he whispered into her hair as he cupped her ass, helping her squirm closer to him...closer to the edge.

"Is that what I'm doing? It feels different." A ragged laugh burst from her lungs. "It's like you've been reincarnated as some badass version of the boy I knew. You're so familiar. And...not."

"I'm not that person anymore." He repeated what he'd told her earlier.

"I know. And neither am I. But you've improved and I'm..." She stopped short of admitting how broken she felt.

"You're amazing." Leaning in, he nuzzled their noses together. This close, she could spy the ice-blue flecks between the gray of his irises. "Don't make me show you."

"What if I want you to?" she whispered. Never in her life had she needed that confirmation more than this instant.

"Are you sure?" His breath ghosted across her lips. "Do you know what you're asking for?"

"Not really," she admitted. "But I want you to show me. Whether that makes me a fool or not. *This* is for me."

"I wish I'd earned every bit of your confidence." He groaned and slipped closer, his lips brushing hers as he spoke. "But I thank you for it anyway. And I'm enough of a bastard to take what you're offering. Because I've wanted it for half my life. I never thought I'd see you again, Kaelyn. I never thought I'd find out what you taste like beyond that pathetic nibble I had."

With that admission, her heart cracked. Or maybe it reformed itself, slightly stronger than it had been before. She lifted her hands, caressing his neck on the way to burying her fingers in his hair. A tug and a whimper later, her mouth crashed into his.

Doubts vanished. Instinct prevailed. Her lips caressed Bryce's, nudging him to respond when he appeared frozen with either shock or disbelief. Her tongue emerged to flirt with the seam of his lips when he held back. The tension in the muscles that quivered around her proved his restraint. Except she suddenly hoped to rip that away from him. To make him as exposed as she felt in his arms, and in the world in general these past few days.

His roar proved he felt it too, this powerful yearning that ensured she'd never be cold again despite the dampness on her skin. Or maybe the moisture gathering between her thighs, which had nothing to do with the bath she'd abandoned.

For the first time since her neighbor had taken off in the night, never to return home, something inside her stirred. Reawakened. Her craving seemed to have grown from the budding interest she'd experienced for her teenaged friend to a full-on blaze of desire for the man he'd turned into.

Kaelyn didn't give a crap that it wasn't ladylike when she coiled her legs around his hips and smothered him like the mink coat she'd hated, doubly so since her father had insisted she wear it in the company of his peers. Bryce didn't seem to mind. She devoured his lips as they softened against hers. Soon she found herself being rocked backward beneath the force of his returned affection.

She'd been in the driver's seat, but only for a moment.

Thank God.

The Bryce she'd sensed beneath his calm exterior showed up, proud and insistent. He grappled with her, squishing her closer to the furnace of his core until the thickness of his hard cock beneath his jeans rode the bare, sensitive place at the apex of her thighs. She squeaked and maybe jerked at the initial contact.

Not because she hoped for escape. But because she'd been unprepared for the shock he sent through her system. Everything screamed out in response, begging for more of that pure electricity. White-hot radiance stole everything from her mind except thoughts of how to ride the lightning he forked through her veins.

Worries disappeared, replaced by unadulterated lust.

In two seconds, he'd reinforced her objections to the quiet, pleasant loving that hadn't done much for her when she'd been intimate with her previous boyfriends.

Freedom to explore raged through her, empowering her. She raked her French manicured nails down his chest, sad for the tiny bit of space insinuated between her and the wall of muscles in front of her, which made her feel protected by their inherent strength. So she slid her hands around his ribs, reveling in how they bellowed with the force of his escalating respiration.

The nonverbal admission of her effect on him turned her on even more.

Kaelyn hugged him to her despite the fact that she had to break contact with his mouth to suck in a gasping breath. He took the opportunity to kiss her chin and jaw, working toward her ear. Who knew it could be so sensitive there?

A soft moan escaped her when he progressed to her neck and had her quaking in his unrelenting grasp. Thankfully, he seemed only to gain strength and momentum as he feasted on her tender flesh while she turned malleable in his hands.

Her spine arched, granting him access to anything he chose to sample. From her collarbone then downward to the curve of her modest breasts. Never before had she regretted her lack of endowment. But his hands made her seem tiny when he cupped her, rolling her hardened nipples between his fingers while staring at the darkening peaks as if they were the most fascinating things he'd ever seen.

"Beautiful," he murmured.

And before she could figure out what to say, he'd descended on them, flicking his tongue over first one, then the other. She gasped and speared her fingers into his hair once more, using the grip to mash him closer while steadying herself against the dizziness encroaching. He had her completely off-balance, her entire world shifting beneath her with the talented swipes of his tongue.

Her toes curled behind his back, where her ankles crossed, hugging him to her.

Could this really be happening?

Sure, she'd had plenty of dreams that ended up like this. Some plain old fantasies too. Daydreams. Lots of them. Well, except Bryce hadn't had these tattoos, or been so muscular, and they'd been in a bed, not on the bathroom sink.

Beggars couldn't be choosers.

And she was certainly about to plead if he didn't start sucking her harder, pulling her nipple into his hot, moist mouth.

As if he listened to her silent demands, he increased the pressure of his suckling, tugging on her distended peaks until he drew her more fully between his lips. His tongue danced around the tissue while his hand entertained her other breast.

When he released her with a slick noise that probably shouldn't have sent shockwaves through her core, she whimpered. Quick to stifle her complaints, he switched sides, balancing out his decadent treatment.

His free hand wandered down her stomach, causing her to suck in a breath and drop her head back against the mirror with a decided *thunk*. Oops.

Bryce chuckled around her breast, peeking up at her to ensure she was okay before proceeding with his dexterous handling of her most sensitive parts.

He winked up at her, then proceeded to circle her belly button with barely there brushes of his index finger. His mouth abandoned her in favor of blazing a trail of kisses that followed the path of his hand.

He kissed her ribs, then her stomach, pausing to lick the swells of her hipbones. And when his chin nudged her mound, she flung her hands to the edge of the countertop and clung as tight as she could manage to keep from rocketing into orbit or plunging to the tile floor. The entire world seemed to wobble beneath her.

Kaelyn's eyes drifted closed as she focused on the pleasure Bryce imparted with every connection of his body to hers. Soft touches, licks, nuzzles and the warm puff of happy sighs buffeted the delta between her legs.

The air swirling over her pussy turned cooler as Bryce inhaled deeply, seeming to savor the scent of her arousal, which he'd inspired. She peeked at him. Meeting his gaze as he stared up at her, as if waiting for permission.

She nodded as best she could with every nerve in her body humming.

Then it was more than a breeze washing over her. His mouth found her, again blanketing her in reverent kisses that swirled closer and closer to her clit. Though she'd gotten herself off hundreds of times, it felt foreign and divine when Bryce arrowed in on the pulsing bundle of nerves and licked once, long and slow.

Montgomery Price had never been up for contact that crass. Or that satisfying.

Kaelyn mewled, trying not to screech and draw his friends down on them again as she had when the sparkles had exploded on her in the bath. Somehow the glitter seemed appropriate now, as if demonstrating the twinkle he put in every cell of her being with his expert playing of her body.

His hands spread her knees apart farther, the stretch adding to the delicious sensations bombarding her. Wet noises echoed in the tiled bathroom as he burrowed into the moist folds of her pussy and ate her with gusto. There were no polite, dainty nibbles of delicacies here. No sipping with raised pinkies. He slurped and savored her without a care for decorum.

She appreciated his enthusiasm as he spiraled her higher and higher, lifting her arousal beyond measure. A tremble began in her toes and worked its way along her body until she shivered in his grasp, her hips arcing upward to meet his attentive mouth, lifting her ass from the vanity with regular pumps.

Lost in the moment, she didn't care how desperate she might appear. Or how wanton. Vulnerable.

With one hand propped behind her, elbow locked, she used the other to curl around his neck and draw him deeper into her core. The increased contact had her thighs trembling around his face. Her knees knocked against his shoulders, which they draped over.

He teased her, drawing quick circles around her clit before sucking on it then repeating the pattern. Though she'd like this euphoria to last forever, nothing so brilliant could be long-lived.

Especially not when he wormed a hand between them to trace the clenching opening of her pussy. She bucked upward, trying to lodge him within her, but he resisted her at first. Teasing, dipping barely inside before retreating.

A tortured moan left her as the ache he built within her began to throb.

As if realizing he'd pushed her to the brink, he granted her relief. When he slid a finger inside her, then two, stretching the walls of her pussy, she didn't stand a chance at resisting his invasion. Into her body or into her heart. Okay, so he'd taken up residence there years ago and his memory had never left, even when she'd thought him gone.

Forever out of reach.

Overwhelming emotions—gratefulness, relief, joy, heartbreak, ecstasy—combined into a cocktail that had her drunk on the pleasure Bryce fed her.

He curled his digits, pumping them into her as he rubbed the front wall of her pussy, hitting a spot she hadn't known she possessed. He triggered so many parts of her only he could reach, and in doing so granted her release.

Kaelyn shattered beneath the potent onslaught.

She came with great, wracking shudders that bordered on sobs.

Bryce allowed her to ride them out, maximizing the potential of each clench with the magic movements of his hands even as he stood to look her in the eye while she continued to unravel.

Before she could disintegrate fully, she reached for the top button of his jeans. The fabric strained beneath the pressure of his erection, which was clearly visible through the pants that conformed to every inch of his package and ass. Her thumb rubbed the wet spot at the top of the impressive bulge.

He raised a brow at her, monitoring her reaction. A hint of uncertainty crept into his gaze as he watched her fall apart. He brushed her fingers aside before they could curl over the waistband of his jeans and soak in his hard heat.

Then, to her horror, her gasps really did morph into blubbering. From the epic orgasm he'd given her or something else entirely, she couldn't say.

Too much. She'd gone through too damn much today. Emotions flooded out of the cracks left behind in the wake of her physical shattering. His rejection of her untrained touch was the last straw. In a jerky motion, she tugged her hand free of Bryce's and used it to cover her eyes. Facing him would be impossible now.

His fingers slipped from her still-spasming sheath as he pursued her.

"Hey." He didn't let her retreat very far. Instead he put his arms around her, treating her as if she were a fragile vase. So different from the authority of his passionate touch, which she'd experienced just moments ago. She hated the change.

Thrashing, she tried to break away. He refused to let her budge.

"Calm down, Kae. I don't want you busting your ass off this counter. It's okay. I've got you. And you don't have to...you know...reciprocate. I only wanted to give you something. A little peace. Something good after everything bad that happened. All right?"

She pressed her face to the crook of his neck and bawled.

"Okay, shit, more like I *had* to do it. I needed to taste you, Kae. I'm sorry if it was too much, too soon. You've had a hell of a week. I shouldn't have pushed you like that, lady." He kept rambling apologies that she couldn't communicate to him were unnecessary through her tears.

Couldn't he tell how much he'd given her?

Fear and anxiety bled from her like poison streaming from a wound.

His generous caring cleansed her.

"It was p-perfect." She hiccupped as she finally got the strength to grant him some reassurance. "It's just. A lot. Everything. Different. New."

"What do you mean *new*?" He would have to latch onto that, wouldn't he?

She didn't respond right away. Her spine straightened and she pushed back from him a bit.

"Kae, answer me." The stern request sent another shock through her system. "You said you weren't a virgin."

Calm down, already, would you? she scolded her body.

"I'm not. I've had sex before." She considered fudging. How could she when she'd settle for nothing but the pure truth from him anymore? "But I've never felt anything like *that* before."

"Like what?" The smarmy grin tugging at his glistening lips tempted her recent resolve. She cleared her throat and attempted to repay him for the rapture he'd gifted her with. This time the heat staining her cheeks had more to do with embarrassment than desire.

"Like I'd die if I didn't come. Or like I could do that forever without my mind wandering to the charity event I'm planning next. Like I'd die happy if I could do that and nothing else for the next decade." She figured she could stop there though there was so much more rushing through her.

"Glad to hear it." He chuckled as he swooped in for a kiss, calling quits before it got too intense. Still it was long enough for her to sample their mingled flavors and decide she liked it. "Because I sure as hell have never eaten anyone as sweet as you. I'm going to need another taste soon."

"So why won't you let me touch you?" She tilted her head, scrutinizing his wince.

"Because if you do, I'll lose control. And you're not ready for that. For me. Not today. Not with everything else going on." He cleared his throat. "I shouldn't have pressed you. I didn't mean for this to happen. Not now. And not like this."

"I'm glad it did." She offered him a shy smile as her body hummed its approval. Warm and liquid, she settled into a delicious afterglow. "I've waited long enough to experience the kind of passion I've read about, don't you think?"

"You and me both." He grinned.

"And I've learned not to take things for granted." She took a deep breath. "I should have told you when we were kids how much you meant to me. I regretted that the most once you were gone."

"Same goes, lady." He covered her face in butterfly kisses, showing her he understood.

Maybe even felt the same. "You have no idea how much I've missed you."

"And now that I know how people can disappear from your life, I don't want to ever waste a chance." She blurted out what had been bugging her since before he crashed her solo bath party. "But I don't want to put you or your friends in danger. I should leave. The sooner the better."

"Shush. You're not going anywhere, Kae." He hugged her so tight she might have squeaked if she could have drawn the breath for it. "Not until this is resolved. The gang agrees. Each of us came here running from something. Hot Rods has been our sanctuary. We'd never shut the door on someone who needs shelter. Stay and figure this out. I'll help you."

"And then?" She hated that she asked, but now that she'd found him, the thought of losing him again shredded her guts.

"That's up to you." Part of her still worried maybe he was being polite, offering her a place until she got on her feet. She sighed, swallowed hard and forced herself to separate from him. Put a modicum of distance between them. Getting too attached was something she couldn't afford.

"Okay?" He glanced down at her, concern in his stormy gray eyes as he swiped the last drops of moisture from her cheeks with his thumbs.

She nodded, unable to speak. Or at least afraid of what her voice might convey.

Bryce plucked her towel from the floor, where it had fallen. Utterly forgotten. He tucked her in the warm, soft fabric, then linked their fingers and led her toward the bathroom door.

"Want me to ask Sally or Nola for some PJs?" He winced as he glanced over his shoulder from their joined hands to her towel-dress, which couldn't begin to hide the lovely rose and lilac marks he'd left on her with his love bites.

"Nah. At this point it seems kind of silly." She grinned, not one bit sorry for what they'd done or how today had turned out. From the lowest point in her life to a record high, she couldn't have traded up any better.

He nodded and grinned, a hint of the boy he'd been shining through his tough-guy exterior. She squeezed his hand before he led her into the hall.

Where several of the Hot Rods were milling around. Had they heard her cries as Bryce ate her out? How could they have missed them?

Instead of mortification, Kaelyn felt pride in Bryce and his ability to please her.

No other man had managed that feat.

If the way his chest puffed out was any indication, shame didn't enter the equation for him either. His friends stared as they made their way through the crowd, presumably toward Bryce's room. Kaelyn couldn't help but think they eyed her like a pack of dogs would a thick, juicy steak.

So why didn't that bother her either?

"Hey! Eyes over here, assholes," Bryce barked at his friends, drawing their notice, if not as quickly as he might have liked. Holden tossed her a wink before he gave their rebel his full attention.

And that was when his eyes grew wide and a decidedly evil chuckle burst from his seriously impressive chest. Cut and trim, he could have been a model. For something sinful as well as sexy. Alcohol, or underwear, or maybe chocolate.

She shook her head. Bryce had put her hormones into overdrive if she was thinking of his friends like that. Especially after the release he'd granted her not a minute ago.

The matching laugh from Alanso had her refocusing. What was so funny?

"You're fucking blinding me, Rebel." Holden ribbed Bryce. "What's with the glitter in your beard? Is that some new fashion statement? Or did you forget to wipe your face after dessert?"

"Asshole." Bryce reached for Swinger, but the smaller guy had agility on his side. When Kaige shuffled closer, Bryce seemed to regain his composure.

Kaelyn took one hand off the knot of her towel to pat his back. Surprised at the tension coiling his muscles, she stiffened.

"Don't worry, Kae." He looked at her, then rolled his eyes. "They're jealous, that's all."

"Damn fucking straight." Holden crossed his arms, making the ink splashed across his pecs stand out even more. What did these guys have against shirts? "You know I prefer to eat buffet-style. Funny, I thought you did too. Maybe Meep's right. You're not the guy we've bonded with."

Could he mean...? No, she had to have misunderstood.

Kaelyn stared at Swinger. So she saw Kaige punch him in the arm. Not hard enough to do any significant damage to his sturdy build, but enough to break up whatever current had arced between him and Bryce for an instant.

She must have imagined it.

Because soon the roughhousing had deteriorated into a wrestling match and the rest of the gang took sides and cheered. A couple even seemed like they were making bets, until Nola busted up the ruckus.

By then, no one was looking at Kaelyn or Bryce.

He took advantage of the distraction to tug her into his room and slam the door.

What had put him in such a foul mood? The Bryce she knew had been even-tempered, silver-tongued and well-mannered. Who was he now?

Who was she after today?

She had a feeling they were both about to discover something new. Maybe who they'd become...together. A girl could dream.

CHAPTER FIVE

Bryce handed Kaelyn his Hot Rods T-shirt, a sample Nola had designed as part of the merchandise line they were launching for the shop. The badass car in the center burst through a ring of stars with a cityscape in the background that had each of the mechanics' names spearing out like the spokes on a wheel, and the slogan *Live Free, Ride Hard* beneath it. If it hadn't already been his favorite before tonight, it would have instantly elevated to that status after draping Kae's svelte curves. The way it hugged her breasts and flared around her hips, leaving her ridiculously long legs exposed, had him shuffling into the closet, pretending to riffle through his wardrobe to hide his raging erection from her too-keen gaze.

After tasting her, it'd taken every scrap of his willpower not to fuck her senseless. And himself as well. But something told him she wasn't quite ready for that. Her innocent fumbling for his pants had nearly undone him while setting off warning alarms in his brain that simultaneously made him cheer and groan. Despite her protests, she wasn't like the women he'd brought home from bars, forward and greedy. Something was off, however hot she'd been. He vowed to take things as slow as he could. That wouldn't mean much for a Hot Rod, born to speed and love every second. Hopefully it would be enough for his princess.

When he turned around, he found Kaelyn staring at his mirror. At first he thought she was eyeing the outrageous proof of his aggression on her reflection. Bite rings, hickeys, whisker burn, you name it. He'd marked her with every tool he had at his disposal. Seeing her like that made it clear, even if it had been subconscious at the time.

And then he realized that wasn't her focus.

Kaelyn stretched out her hand and touched a battered photograph tucked into the frame of the mirror. It'd been there so long it was one of those things that had become part of the backdrop of his room instead of an element he consciously recalled.

It might also be the reason Kaige had thought Kaelyn looked familiar when Bryce had carried her inside earlier today.

The picture was the only fragment of his history that he'd taken when he left.

"I remember this like it was yesterday." The mirror reflected her smile. Solemn and full of regrets compared to the wide, brilliant version she'd worn in the selfie they'd taken less than twenty-four hours before he'd fled. "I never saw the picture, since it was on your phone. And you…left…that night—"

She paused as if she couldn't quite believe that they'd met again in this lifetime. Reunited on Earth, not in Heaven…or Hell. Bryce wasn't sure yet where he'd spend eternity, though disappointing her certainly made him feel like a sinner.

Fuck, he couldn't quite grasp the concept either. Never mind that he'd sampled paradise between her legs. Their entire reality had changed—history rewritten. That would take a while to get used to. For them both.

Bryce walked up behind her and wrapped her in his arms, trying to still the fine trembling that overtook her again. He glanced at them in the mirror, loving the image they made together. So different than the innocents that stared from the creased photo below their live reflection.

Yet still the same in a lot of ways.

Her, so beautiful it made his heart hurt.

Him, hiding things—this time it was the details of the life he'd built here—and still not good enough for her.

"It was a good day. One of the best," Bryce whispered in her ear. "I loved that ride we took in my car. Way out into the countryside. I remember how much you squealed while looking at the horses running free on the ranchland while I navigated the curves in the winding road."

"Way too fast." She smiled as she scolded him.

"I never risked you. Believe me, had I been alone I would have taken them at twice that speed." He nuzzled her neck. "Reckless wasn't in my vocabulary when it came to you."

"Maybe if it had been you would have done more than picnic with me on that blanket you'd tucked into the trunk." She leaned into his caresses. "I enjoyed the food we ate under that huge oak tree while we watched the horses in the valley below, but I might have liked you making out with me on the hood of the Maserati better."

He groaned. "You're the only woman I'd consider that with, you know. Now, anyway. Back then you were too damn young. Completely innocent. Look at you."

They both glanced to the picture. Youthful versions of themselves smiled back. Oblivious to how close they were to the shattering of their lives. Or maybe the beginning of new ones.

Better for Bryce.

Worse for Kae.

"If I had it to do over again, I'd take you with me," he confessed.

"If I knew then what I know now, I'd have looked for you. I wouldn't have quit until I hunted you down." She accepted some of the blame, which she didn't deserve, for their separation. Kaelyn blanketed his fingers with her hand and squeezed. "My life was never the same without you. No one understood me like you did. No one...encouraged me to try things or see new places like you had. I quit planning my sweet-sixteen trip after you vanished. I figured if you'd wanted to show me around Europe like you'd sworn, you would call. And if not, I didn't want to see the place you loved more than—"

She practically deflated in his hold.

He cursed into her hair, wishing he had been there to chaperone the wild adventures they'd fantasized about. But if he had stayed, she never would have been safe. Neither of them would have been.

Those chances had been stolen from him as certainly as he'd been taken from her.

Maybe he could make it up to her. Give her some of the experiences they'd both missed out on. *Yeah, like eating her until you both pass out from sheer bliss.*

Well, in some ways it was a start.

His thick cock nudged Kaelyn's pert ass, making her blink her pretty blue eyes at him.

Bryce separated them a bit and reached up to rub the knot in his lower neck, which had him wincing. The damn thing always gave him fits when he was stressed. Of course Kae noticed.

"What's wrong?" she asked.

"Nothing important." He rolled his shoulders, trying to dislodge some of the tension invading him at being so near her yet unable to claim her. Yet. "I get this kink sometimes from the hours I spend on the creeper, under cars. The board's not really big enough for me. My shoulder hangs off the edge, so it gets cramped sometimes. Don't worry."

He skirted the truth, leaving out the part about how the lust balled in him was amplifying any strain caused by the undersized device he used for work.

She nudged him toward the bed. "Lie down on your stomach. Let me rub it. I've had enough massages at the spa to maybe figure this out."

No way would he pass up the chance to have her hands on him. Preferably on his cock, but anywhere would do for now. He rambled to keep from freaking her out. Hopefully, she couldn't tell how desperate he was for her touch.

"We have a friend…" How to explain the Powertools crew, Bryce wondered. "Well, a bunch of friends that are kind of a clan of their own. Like the Hot Rods. But they're a construction crew."

She didn't have to know *how* alike they were. Not yet.

"Anyway, one of the crew wives—Kayla—is a masseuse. When she gets the spot right it doesn't hurt for like two weeks after. It's amazing." He paused when he realized Kae hadn't followed him onto the mattress. He glanced over his shoulder to see her standing there with a funny look on her face.

"What?" he asked.

"Are you trying to make me jealous?" She surprised him by jogging the few steps to the bed, then jumping on it. "Telling me about some woman with magic hands? Is she pretty? Does she turn you on when she's petting you?"

Bryce laughed out loud. "I like you green, lady. There's nothing for you to get wired up about. Kayla is happily married to my friend

Dave. She's not like the socialite bitches we knew who'd cuckold their husbands for the sport of it."

And she's bonded to the rest of her husband's partners, not to mention their wives. But that was a story for another day, he figured.

Hopefully she wouldn't hold the omission against him.

"Ah, perfect." She grinned. "Then maybe sometime she could teach me so you never have to suffer again."

Both of them grew quiet and still.

"I mean, for as long as I'm around, anyway," Kaelyn amended quietly.

"Does that mean you've forgiven me?" He held his breath while she took her time responding.

"I'm still angry. With my father, yours, you, life in general. But I'd be lying if I said I wasn't glad to be here. Or if I denied the attraction between us." She took a deep breath. "So, as long as I'm welcome, I'm going to take you up on your offer. And while I'm here, I'd like to explore what's between us."

He might have reassured her that he didn't plan to let her fly away anytime soon if she hadn't chosen then to put her hands on him and begin rubbing. As she straddled his ass, the damp heat of her—bare since she wore nothing beneath his lucky T-shirt—pressed to his lower back, reminding him of how hot and wet she'd been on his face. His boner tucked uncomfortably beneath him as if it attempted to bore into the mattress. What he wouldn't have given to flip over, tumble Kae onto the bed and fuck her senseless, like both of them longed for.

Except he was sure she needed some time to adjust even more than she needed to come apart. That didn't stop his cock from trying to convince him that everyone loved a good orgasm or twenty when they were wound up.

Before Bryce's libido could talk him into a bad decision, Kaelyn drew his attention again.

This time he realized that in addition to kneading his sore shoulder, which simultaneously hurt like a motherfucker and relaxed beneath her caresses, she was tracing his ink. He should have considered what she might think about his back piece.

"You hated your old life this much?" Her hard swallow was audible in the quiet space.

Tom's advice came back to him in a rush. *Don't let her think you despised her.*

Her hands ran over the stacks of flaming money that paved the way to hell as it snaked across his back. Corruption, greed and gluttony made demons that ripped at the angelic mechanics above in a parody—or maybe his own interpretation—of Michelangelo's Last Judgment from the altar wall of the Sistine Chapel.

In the center, it was his hand, reaching for Tom's—the man who'd saved him along with his Hot Rod brothers and sister—in a blending of the Creation of Adam with Bryce's life. Though he'd stopped thinking of his garagemates as siblings since they'd transitioned their bond into something deeper, something sexual, he'd never stopped acknowledging the gang as his saviors. Without them, he would have been doomed.

He let Kaelyn explore his past and the depiction of his rebirth. She paused when she got to her own likeness, etched on his shoulder in the form of an angel. After scrutinizing the picture he'd given the artist to work from, she couldn't mistake his intent. Or the proof of his undying admiration for her. Her fingers traced the rays shining from her surreal figure. He hoped she realized that's how he saw her. Ideal. Otherworldly in her beauty. Then and twice as much now.

Pure perfection.

Clearing his throat he said, "There were some things I could never hate. Kae, you might have come from that world, but you never belonged either. I don't count you as part of the evil I left behind. I'm so sorry I couldn't think of some way to bring you with me. To save you too."

She surprised him when she laid a kiss over the part of the tattoo he thought of as himself. Gentle as a whisper, he might have thought he imagined it if every nerve ending of his body wasn't tuned to her frequency.

"It's beautiful, Bryce." She walked her fingers lower to the Hot Rods logo on the side of his torso, over his ribs. "I always wanted a tattoo. Another thing on the list of stuff I never got around to after you abandoned…"

He grunted. "It's okay to keep thinking that, Kae. I *did*."

She patted the resurrection depicted in his tattoo.

They both deserved a new start. She was gracious enough to grant him one.

"Well, anyway, I guess I let a bunch of my ambitions slip through the cracks. I didn't go after the things we'd dreamed about. I couldn't face it on my own." She sighed. "I wasted a lot of time. If I hadn't been so…"

"Lost," he whispered.

"Yeah, I guess. If I hadn't given up, I might have escaped on my own before this whole fiasco." She sounded so bitter, he had to turn over and tug her into his arms. Willingly, she stretched out beside him and cuddled into his chest, with her cheek resting above his heart.

"Kaelyn, I'm sorry to say this, but..." Bryce considered hedging then decided she deserved the truth from him always. She was strong enough to hear it. "If you'd rebelled, they'd have tried to squash you. It was only because you went along with their plans that they left you alone. Of that I'm sure now."

"What makes you say that?" She lifted up enough to meet his gaze.

"Tom told me he has evidence that my father..." He choked on the confession.

"That he *what*?" She grew still in his arms, waiting for him to spit it out.

"That my mom tried to divorce him, and he made sure she couldn't tarnish his reputation. He kicked her out, in the middle of winter. That's how she got sick. He snuffed her mutiny, Kaelyn, like everything else that refuses to bow to his demands." Bryce bit his lip, wishing he could have rescued her too. "Your dad is the same way. It's why they're such tough opponents. They're exactly alike underneath the pandering and the lies."

Kaelyn patted his chest, helping to neutralize some of the acid building within his gut. She knew how to calm him, how to help him vent. She always had. Like the time she stopped him from punching some kid whose name he couldn't even remember anymore for claiming his mother had committed suicide to get away from him and his dad. Probably not too far from the truth, he was willing to admit these days.

Probably why he'd boiled over at the suggestion.

Kaelyn had sauntered between them and asked him to take her for a ride, coming up with some excuse that hadn't mattered.

Even then, driving had been his one reprieve.

"I can't believe you kept my car, Kae." He didn't even try to stop himself from running his fingers through the platinum stands of her hair. So soft. So long.

"It was the one thing I never understood. Why you left it at my house. I figured you'd got something newer, flashier, to replace it with when you never had it shipped overseas. Your dad didn't ask for it. Maybe he just didn't care, but I figured he knew as well as me you weren't coming back or you would have made sure it was in your garage, buttoned up and babied like you always did before." She sighed. "On days when I missed you more than I hated you for ditching me, I'd get in it and drive. Or just sleep in it."

Her cheek heated beneath his knuckles as he swiped away another tear from her crystalline eyes.

"You should take it. It's yours." She sniffled.

"I like thinking of you behind the wheel. In control and confident. Sexy and fast." He hummed, willing his erection not to make a comeback at the thought. "Keep it. Things were always more important to you anyway."

"What's that supposed to mean?" She stiffened in his grip, putting space between them. He hated that gap and tugged her back into place, draped over him.

"Only that I thought you enjoyed creature comforts. You're not going to be able to come by them so easily anymore. You'd better hang on to what you can." He groaned. "Or sell it. I can help you line up a buyer and negotiate a fair deal. Things are going well here at the shop. Better lately than I could have imagined. But I can't provide everything your dad could have."

"He couldn't give me the one thing that mattered." Kaelyn stared him down, revving his engine even more with the slightly pissed-off stare she flung in his direction. "Don't think I don't know the value of love, Bryce. Don't think I wouldn't trade that other junk in a second for the real thing. I think that's why it was so easy for Montgomery to deceive me."

"I still can't believe you fell for a guy named Montgomery. He even sounds like a douche." Bryce snorted, hoping to distract her from her ire with his sense of humor. She used to prefer laughing to fighting anyway.

She slapped him, but giggled. "Well, I thought I did. I should have known what I felt was only a shadow of what could be."

Kaelyn looked away then.

"I've seen love firsthand." Bryce spoke soft and slow, afraid of how much he might reveal. "All you have to do is spend a few minutes around Eli, Sally and Alanso or Kaige and Nola to feel how hot it burns. The real thing. There's no mistaking that."

He felt like a hypocrite when he ignored the inferno turning his heart to cinders for the woman splayed over him. But so much had happened, so soon, he was afraid to scare her with what he suspected. He'd detected that same devotion in his eyes when he caught his reflection in the bathroom mirror while he'd feasted on her and again while they'd visited their younger selves in the photograph.

"Yeah, I could see that earlier." She nodded and bit her lip. "Just, don't assume I'm like everyone else from our world, okay? You know I'm not. Or at least you used to."

Maybe he'd tried to convince himself she needed posh things to assuage his guilt over having to desert her. It'd been easier when he thought she couldn't survive in his new life.

One full of hard work and dedication. It wouldn't be everyone's first choice, though he thrived in the environment.

"I'll keep that in mind, lady." He tugged a lock of her hair, thrilled when a smile etched into the corners of her luscious mouth. For the first time in a long time, he saw her dimples flash up at him and his restraint nearly disintegrated like a rusty muffler on a bumpy road.

Bryce cupped her chin in his palm and directed her toward his mouth. He lay as still as possible when she accepted his invitation and placed a series of featherlight kisses on his lips. He groaned and clenched her hips to keep from wresting control from her.

After all that had happened, he sensed her need for some power. Little did she know, she had him wrapped around her pinky. Or maybe some other choice parts of her magnificent anatomy.

Kaelyn climbed him, settling her mouth more firmly on his as she aligned their bodies.

No way could she miss his arousal. Neither did she seem put off by the thick ridge of his cock, which she began to sinuously glide against as she devoured his wicked grin.

His hands roamed down to her ass, cupping her and encouraging her to ride him to both their delights. The bare flesh of her pussy heated him through the sweats he'd changed into and he groaned into her mouth.

Thinking of how fast he could have his pants off and a condom sheathing his rock-hard erection, he didn't hear the knock at the door at first.

Kaelyn's guilty look and the jump she took off him onto the mattress was his first clue. By the time she dove beneath his comforter, covering her nude legs and bare pussy, he'd become aware of some of his surroundings. More than Kaelyn and her infectious hunger anyway.

A light rap came again.

"Who is it?" he barked.

"Sally." She cracked open the door and peered in with big doe eyes that couldn't fool him. She was no innocent. The nosey woman glanced between them, seeming almost disappointed when she noticed their clothes and the distance separating them. "I brought you some leftover pizza and a couple beers. We thought you might have worked up an appetite while you were getting to know each other again."

Bryce glanced at the clock on his night table, surprised to see how late it had gotten. It seemed time flew when Kaelyn was near. His stomach growled in response.

Kaelyn and Sally laughed at him as Mustang transferred a pizza box and a bucket of beer into Bryce's clutches. Kae, pizza and beer—he was as happy as Buster McHightops in a mud puddle with those three things in his bed.

"I'll get out of your hair, just wanted to see how everything's going."

"It was pretty great until you interrupted," Bryce grumbled as he leaned his shoulders against the headboard. "But I appreciate dinner. Thanks for thinking of Kaelyn when I was…distracted."

"Anytime." Sally winked as she backed toward the door. "Well, you two enjoy. Don't expect we'll see you before the morning so…sleep tight. Or not."

A lyrical chuckle followed her out the door. Bryce wished he could spank her for her good-natured prying. But that would require a heck of a lot of explaining.

He glanced at Kaelyn, who peeked into the box.

"Something wrong?" He joined her under the covers, scooting closer so that their thighs rested along each other, instantly heating where they touched.

"There are no plates. Or napkins. Or cups." She glanced around as if the contents of the kitchen cabinets would suddenly appear.

"You're an honorary Hot Rod now, lady. You're going to have to rough it." Bryce reached across her and twisted off the cap of a beer before handing it to her. She probably had champagne tastes. Still, she didn't wrinkle her nose when she took a big gulp.

Flipping back the lid of the pizza box, Bryce pulled her closer so that they could eat slices over the greasy cardboard simultaneously. Their impromptu picnic seemed to grow on Kaelyn as she forgot about dirtying his sheets and dug into the gooey delight.

Soon they were laughing like they had when they were kids chowing down on a piece of birthday cake they'd stolen away to her tree house, filling up on stringy cheese and slugging down beers. Bryce could honestly say he'd never been as attracted to Kae as he was when she looked over and licked red sauce straight from her fingers. When she sucked on her thumb, he just about had a heart attack. They passed the rest of the evening with laughter and stories. Catching up on where they'd been, the people he'd known and learning what each other liked these days. Most of the fundamentals hadn't changed. She was still the girl he'd adored under that womanly grace and charm.

"So…I probably should have asked sooner, but you don't have a girlfriend, do you? I told you about Montgomery. Have you had someone…special?" She seemed horrified by the idea as she rolled onto her side on his pillows and squinted at him.

"Nah." He shrugged, though hesitating as he wondered what she'd call the Hot Rods. Sure, he slept with them, Mustang Sally and Nola included, but it wasn't like they were his. They were Eli's and Kaige's women. Alanso's too. Lent to him for their pleasure and his own.

"Why don't you sound certain about that?" She sat up, nibbling her lower lip. "I assumed, after what happened in the bathroom."

Her pink skin turned an unhealthy shade of green as she probably drummed up some horrible scenario that had them both cheating on an imaginary woman in her mind.

"Kaelyn, I promise, I'm not tied down. I don't have anyone of significance." So why did that feel like a lie? He tried to explain as best he could without breaking his friends' confidence. He'd have to talk to them. Soon. About what to share. How much. How soon. And what Kaelyn's presence meant for them going forward.

Except he didn't know.

The thought of pulling away from the group socked him in the gut, stealing his breath. He remembered what it had been like the night of Eli, Alanso and Sally's wedding, watching Kaige walk away with Nola. He didn't want to do that. Not to himself or to his friends. But it was a lot to ask of Kaelyn, especially when he knew she didn't have a lot of bedroom miles on her.

"Okay." She settled again, snuggling into his pillows, looking so adorable he wanted nothing more than to smother her with kisses.

"So...before, when you said you don't have a lot of experience with guys." He cleared his throat, needing to know what speed to set his cruise control for. "What exactly does that mean?"

She rolled to her back and studied the ceiling for so long he thought she might not answer.

So he reached across the bed and entangled his fingers with hers, giving them a squeeze to let her know he wasn't about to judge. Still it shocked him when she came clean.

"Sex is boring." She took her free hand and covered her eyes as if it was too much to bear looking at him as she confessed. "I've pretty much explored on my own. With vibrators and stuff, you know. But...with a guy? Yeah, it's more trouble than it's worth. The awkwardness, the pretending it's great, the ego stroking. Eh, I can get myself off in a fraction of the time and go about my day on my own. A much better plan, I think."

Bryce nearly choked on his tongue. "You were engaged. How could you agree to marry a man you weren't passionate about?"

"Uh, well, I think we both know a guy like Montgomery only wanted me as a trophy." She huffed out a sigh. "He probably had some side action for sport. When we made love, he was...so damn polite. I never could lose myself in the moment. Heck, it was more like asking someone to pass the salt at the dinner table when you really want to pour on a gallon of hot sauce, you know? I tried to be adventurous, but he was vanilla to the core. And that didn't do it for me. So I quit pushing for more and took care of myself. I could see us being one of those couples, like people in a '50s TV show who have separate beds."

Bryce figured that was a fate worse than death. Freezing yourself in a cold partnership when there were so many amazing ways to blaze. The Hot Rods had shown him that. He could think of only one reason Kaelyn would settle. "You were scared to look for better, weren't you?"

Tears glistened in her eyes. "I guess. I know what it's like to lose a best friend. Someone who touches me deeply instead of skimming the surface. I couldn't stand to be consumed by that kind of connection again. Montgomery was convenient. Practical. We might have built a pleasant life together if he'd been what he seemed, instead of my dad's crony."

Bryce couldn't say he was sorry. The guy obviously hadn't deserved to touch something as magnificent as her. Still... "Wow. Uh, Kaelyn, I think you should know that I'm thinking pretty dirty thoughts about you. And have been since the second I saw you in that field. Shit, since I was old enough to know what I could do with you. Vanilla's a fine flavor, but I like a hell of a lot more variety than that alone. There's a bunch of spice in my cabinet."

Somehow, admitting his lechery seemed to be the perfect thing. She dropped her hand and beamed over at him. "Seriously?"

With a nod, he grabbed her fingers and slid them to the bulge in his sweats. "Is there really any doubt? I'm a card-carrying freak. And I love that you might be too."

"Bryce," she murmured.

And he knew she was going to torture him with whatever fell out of her pretty lips next.

Because he wasn't sure he could give her what she wanted without taking too much. Was he capable of being gentle enough for a princess like her, one who liked the idea of excitement without having experienced it?

"Yeah, lady?" He manned up and promised himself he'd try.

"I want you to be my first. Like my *real* first. You won't hold back on me, right? I want sex. Super sex. Sweaty, passionate and fierce." She licked her lips, driving him nuts. "Will you f-fuck me?"

Even her stumble over the naughty word turned him on. Bryce took a deep breath and counted to ten so that he could give her time to change her mind. He didn't want to pounce on her and ravish her like the brute he feared he might be instead of the charming prince she'd imagined him as.

"Damn. Sorry. That was ridiculous of me to ask, wasn't it?" She tugged the covers around her, as if anything could prevent him from doing as she requested. "Can we forget I—"

"Hell no, we can't." He growled as he got to his hands and knees and stalked closer. Looming over her on straight-locked arms, he dropped down to nip her neck then worked toward her mouth. Her gasps and soft moans encouraged him as he settled over her.

But part of him wanted to make it as dreamy as he could.

Hell, it was her first *real* time, she deserved some romance. Despite what she thought, he knew genuine adoration was a component of blistering hot attraction. Eli, Alanso and Sally then Kaige and Nola had shown him that. They blended affection and lust into something he'd die to give Kae. He thought of the flowers in the service station downstairs and the soft lighting of his lamp on the bedside table. His iPod was in the living room. In a few minutes he could at least improve on the sparse situation and give her a blend of both.

Plus, he could use a pit stop after sucking down those beers with Kae.

"Hang on. I need a minute if we're going to do this right. I've got to go get some...protection." He mumbled as he tried to engage his big head and silence the little one that screamed at him for letting her escape. Especially when he had condoms in the nightstand drawer. Silly, but he wanted to surprise her, just a bit. "You're welcome to clean up if you want. I know I kind of distracted you before you were finished in the bathroom. Get ready, because I'm not going to pull my punches. You won't be able to sleep through what we're about to share. I promise you that."

"Oh." She blinked up at him as if surfacing from a daze. "Sure. Okay."

It was torture to let her get up and escape the nest they'd made together, the cocoon of reminiscences rehashed mixing with memories they'd make tonight. Part of him panicked at the thought of letting her out of his sight. Afraid of squandering the amazing chemistry they'd enhanced this evening.

"Kaelyn." He couldn't say what possessed him to call her back. Maybe it was the way her fingers trembled on the doorframe. He didn't want her to get the wrong idea.

"Yes?" She swallowed as she looked over at him. Even from across the room, the power of their connection impressed him.

"Hurry back, lady." He winked at her. "I'll be waiting."

The smile she flashed lit up every shadow lingering in his soul. If one simple gesture could illuminate the far reaches of the darkness lurking there, he couldn't wait to see what the fireworks of their joining would do.

To them both.

When she'd slipped into the hall, he jumped into action, turning the lights down low and racing in the opposite direction for the essentials in the other room. No one he bumped into bothered to stop him when they glimpsed the lust and need in his eyes.

Alanso slapped him on the back as he returned with a bouquet, a cheap box of wine and his iPod in tow. Kind of pathetic, but the best he could muster. "Good luck, Rebel."

"Thank you." He raced for his room with the impatience of a teenager after the prom, an event he'd missed and planned to make up for.

Right now.

All night long.

CHAPTER SIX

Kaelyn took a deep breath, thankful for the minute or two alone she had to compose herself before committing to a night of delicious torture. After all, she'd dreamed of sleeping in Bryce's arms a million times. To do more than sleep would be beyond her greatest expectations.

Her hands trembled, rattling the toothbrush someone had set outside the door to Bryce's room in a plastic orange cup with her name scrawled on a piece of masking tape stuck to it. A comb and some other toiletries accompanied the thoughtful present.

Part of her tried not to admit her and Bryce's instantly rejuvenated chemistry and their ultimate lack of decorum on the bathroom sink had flustered her.

But they had.

She'd never experienced *passion* like that before.

Everything in her life had been so sterile, generic. She hadn't realized...

Combined with the evening they'd spent proving that their easy connection hadn't eroded in the nine years they'd been apart, she had no reason to say no to a second, bigger helping of nookie with Bryce.

So when she'd proposed ramping things up for the night, she'd acted as worldly as she dared and shrugged her shoulder as if it would be no big deal to camp out in his bed, which rivaled the size of her canopy bed at home—minus the frills, of course.

Thankful for the excuse of brushing her teeth, she scooted down the hallway. Warm light leaked from beneath the Hot Rods' bedroom doors, leaving the bathrooms dark. She counted as she went, another habit she'd picked up living in a mansion and frequenting others often. On autopilot, her emotions zinged from trepidation to downright lust at the prospect of snuggling tight to the furnace Bryce had made on those cool evenings they'd spent in her tree house.

Hopefully he hadn't lost any of that heat.

Somehow, she knew he hadn't. Heck, he'd practically singed her thighs when he'd buried his face between them earlier. It'd be a million times steamier when it was the thick cock she'd spied tenting his sweatpants filling her instead of his tongue doing the dirty work.

She didn't even dare to think about that without risking spontaneous combustion.

Distracted, Kaelyn lost count. Glancing back then forward, she tried to remember exactly where the bathroom she'd used had been but the hall was long and the doors looked identical as she traveled deeper into the Hot Rods' lair, away from the main living space. She picked the next one with no sign of someone inside. The shadows beneath had her fairly sure she'd reached the bathroom. How would she stare at herself in the mirror long enough to wash up, remembering what had happened there?

Fanning her cheeks with one hand, she reached for the knob. Then paused. She delayed by brushing her hair right there in the hallway, slowly, buying some time. After letting it dry naturally, it took a bit to work the knots loose. Then she had no excuses left.

Don't be so wimpy, she chided herself.

Before she could chicken out, she turned to the bathroom, flung the door open, stepped inside and slapped her hand over the light switch, filling the room with artificial brightness.

Except it wasn't the bathroom.

Oh. My. God.

Candles flickered in the corners of the room, illuminating a decadent scene that put her romp to shame. One man—Carver, she thought—had been tied to a chair. Black nylon rope snaked around his thighs, pinning them wide open before encircling his arms and trapping them as well. A hint of black plastic protruded between his legs, making her wonder what he might be sitting on besides the seat cushion. Whatever it was hadn't kept his cock from standing at full attention, thick and pulsing. Wax coated his ripped and inked chest, making it clear the candles were used for more than illuminating his gorgeous, submissive body.

The meek lovemaking she'd been imagining in her future had nothing on the decadence of the ardor she witnessed as another one of the Hot Rods, Roman, stalked the helpless man, who didn't seem to mind being prey for the sexual marauder hunting him.

"Can you let it go yet, Meep? Or do you need more?" Barracuda urged his partner to relent. "It's in the past. I'm in control now. Of myself. And of you. There's no room here for ghosts. Don't let that old shit ruin what we've built. Bryce isn't your enemy. None of us chose who we were born to. Let it go."

Her eyes grew wide as Roman offered to replace emotional distress with physical sensations, something both men could clearly handle better. She hoped their extreme loving would sear away the damage she'd inadvertently done to their relationship with each other, and their friendship with Bryce.

The man in the chair wriggled, fighting his bonds or trying to exorcise his demons.

Kaelyn figured she knew which it was.

Roman let him struggle, let him rail at the world without being a danger to himself or others. He provided an outlet for his friend's aggression. And seemed to be helping turn Carver's negative energy into something positive. Pleasurable.

They were beautiful as they helped each other through the turmoil the day had rained down on them. *She* had brought pain to them by accident.

A belt unwrapped from around Roman's knuckles as he paced, clad only in leather pants. No wonder they called him Barracuda. His predatory strides captivated her, making her stare. She might even have moaned out loud.

Their heads swiveled toward her intrusion.

A yelp escaped her as she realized that she'd barged in on a *very* private moment. Worse yet, she'd gawked instead of pivoting on her heel and running back out. Heck, she kind of wished they hadn't noticed her so she could have remained mesmerized by their intensity. But they had.

"Holy shipwrecks! I'm sorry." She clapped her hand over her eyes. The gurgling she heard tempted her to peek from between her fingers. Just to make sure Carver was okay, she promised herself.

Instead of struggling to escape, she saw him arching toward Roman, who'd turned toward her—their unwitting intruder. He removed his hand from its task, whatever that might have been, between his partner's legs.

"Swinger. Grab her. Make sure she's okay." Barracuda's commands didn't make sense at first. Until Kaelyn realized that a third man also occupied the space. Holden rose from his perch in the corner—where he'd obviously been enjoying the show. He tucked himself into the gym shorts that had been pooled around his ankles, fast enough to risk injuring the solid hard-on he whisked out of sight. The bulge in the soft fabric did nothing to disguise his impressively erect penis.

Looking away didn't do her any good as her wide gaze landed on Roman, who now stood in front of his immobile roommate. Whether the stance was intended to protect her modesty or his lover's, she couldn't say. Probably both.

"Come on, Kaelyn." Holden paused with his hand a fraction of an inch from her elbow before closing the gap. The warmth of his hold made her shiver for some reason. His tight expression worried her.

Was he angry that she'd stormed into their scene?

Why wouldn't he be? He was missing out on the action by playing chaperone to her.

"I'm sorry," she whispered again around the ball of fire raging inside her. Except the apology was false, or at least she didn't offer it for witnessing what she had. In fact, she wished she could rush back and see what Barracuda had in store for his roommate. That was what she'd been missing. Honest responses to base urges. Perfunctory lovemaking, going through the motions without that raw edge...*that* was what had dulled her eagerness to explore. If Bryce could give her even half that level of engagement, she should sprint to his room and jump him.

Holden grunted. Whether because he was furious or because he dismissed her contrition, she wasn't sure. It could be painful arousal making him brusque since he'd been so rudely interrupted. He marched her toward Bryce's quarters. They hadn't gotten halfway back before his door popped open and he darted into the hallway.

"Is everything okay? I heard a yelp," Bryce asked Swinger, instead of her.

"Fine. I think your girl got lost, though." Kaelyn relaxed when she realized he was chuckling, not seething at her mistake. "She busted in on Roman, Carver and me having some fun. Scoring the room next to a bathroom has its good points and its bad points."

"I'm *so* sorry..." she started again.

He waved her off. "We should have locked the door. It's not exactly a habit around here, though."

Bryce cleared his throat and Holden quit talking. What was he hiding now?

"Well. Here you go." Swinger nudged her lower back, sending her toward Bryce. "If you don't mind, I'm gonna get back to...well, you know."

Kaelyn blushed, but Bryce only nodded.

"You're sure you don't want me to stay and help explain?" Holden winked, or at least she thought he did in the shadowy light.

"Get out of here." A growl from Bryce surprised her. "I can handle this myself."

"If you change your mind..." Swinger turned serious. "Honestly, I mean that. If you could use someone more impartial or just some back up...maybe one of the girls? I could send Sally over in a bit? Or come back to check on you when I'm thinking straight? Have blood flow circulating to the big brain again."

"Thanks." Bryce's broad hands wrung together before he cupped her elbow and turned her toward his room. "We'll manage."

"For the record, babe, you're fucking adorable when you're embarrassed. And *curious*." Whether he added that last part for her or for Bryce's benefit, she couldn't say. He kissed her cheek before darting toward the two guys she'd interrupted. How he jogged with that tent pole in his pants, she had no idea. But he must have wanted to rejoin his buddies pretty badly to endure the discomfort of it bobbing as he ran.

"Well...*that* wasn't how I planned this discussion to go." Bryce tossed her a wry grin then ushered her into his room and closed the door softly behind her. "Honestly, I'd only started worrying about how to bring it up. You kind of saved me some trouble, I think."

On the bed, a laptop sat open and voices jumped out at them. "Yo, Rebel! Everything okay? Where the hell did you go? Who screamed?"

"Ah, shit." Bryce hopped onto the bed, tugging her along with him by their linked fingers. "Sorry. We had a...uh...logistical problem."

"Who are you talking to?" Despite Kaelyn's swirling thoughts and the arousal humming through her, she couldn't help but peek onto the screen where a smattering of men and women peered back at her, equally as inquisitive. She hadn't been gone more than a few minutes. Flowers sat in mason jars on either nightstand and the lights had been doused except for the soft glow of a lamp. Music played in the background and there was a...*videochat*...going on Bryce's laptop.

What the hell?

"Sorry, they called and I wanted to touch base quick. These are our friends. The Powertools gang I mentioned before. Meet Mike, Kate, Dave, Kayla, Morgan, Joe, Devon, Neil and James."

"Wow. There are a lot of them too." She tried to repeat their names in her mind a couple times. At least they didn't have nicknames to keep track of on top of their real ones. Fortunately, she'd spent most of her life at fundraisers, memorizing countless face-name combos that could prove important to her father's success.

The whole day had been a whirlwind, tugging her one way then another. Surprises lurked everywhere and she was starting to get overwhelmed. It was like the truth poured out of her unfiltered after so many bombshells.

"No kidding." Bryce laughed. "Let's just say they've been where Hot Rods are, and they're helping us get our shit together. I thought I had a few minutes to check in with them and let them know about...well, *you*. And our history. My past. I finally feel like I'm not lying to my friends anymore. It feels amazing to get rid of that burden. I hadn't realized how much it still weighed on me."

Kaelyn couldn't stop herself. She laid a hand on his cheek and wished she could erase some of the tension darkening his gorgeous eyes. Surprisingly, her light touch seemed to have some effect. He leaned into her palm and nuzzled it.

"Worry about you, not us," the guy she was pretty sure was named Joe counseled Bryce. "We're not going anywhere. You can call us back later. Or tomorrow, or whenever. After things have settled down. We'll still be right here. But, for the record, I already like what I see."

"Remember, Rebel," Devon, the smallest woman onscreen piped up. "The truth is always your best option. Take this opportunity. I can tell it's going to be okay. You can do this."

"You can share anything with me," Kaelyn promised, stopping short of admitting it wouldn't change her love for the man in front of her. If ten years of believing he had abandoned her hadn't destroyed her feelings, finding out about whatever kinky secrets he and his roommates shared certainly wouldn't either.

She didn't think so anyway. In fact, she was kind of wary that her love for him could turn to *in love* with him someday, if she wasn't careful.

"Okay, we're hanging up now. Good luck, Rebel, though I'm sure you don't need it." Mike waved right before the screen went black.

Bryce carefully closed the laptop and set it aside before taking a breath deep enough to raise his shoulders several inches. She went up behind him and wrapped her arms around his waist, laying her head between his shoulders.

"Can I guess what you're about to say? Will that make it easier on you? I think if I hadn't crashed into your life today, you'd be in that room with your friends. Am I right?" she wondered out loud.

"Probably. Yes." He took it one step further. "Except maybe we'd all be in the living room. With Eli and the rest of the gang too."

"But I didn't get the impression you were gay earlier." Kaelyn didn't mean it as a criticism. She merely struggled to understand the big picture. There'd been no denying his arousal before she'd slipped from beneath him minutes ago. Where did this leave them?

"I'm not." He scrubbed his hands through his hair. "Well, I don't know what I am. What you call it, I mean. I never was attracted to men before them. I like women, though. A hell of a lot. I l-like you, Kae. I want *you*."

"And them too?" She wondered if it bothered her that he was attracted to so many people. Digging deep, she tried not to feel less special than he'd made her seem earlier.

Distress creased the corners of his eyes as he struggled to find the right words.

"Hey, look, you don't have to explain anything to me." She cleared her throat. "I showed up, unannounced, *really* unexpected. You didn't have to take me in. This is none of my business. Maybe we got out of control before. Is that why you needed a minute? To think straight and figure out how to let me down easy? No problem. If you could change my tire, and maybe lend me some gas money, I'll stay out on the couch in the living room. That thing was enormous. And I'll be gone first thing in the morning. Out of your hair before I can screw up what's between—"

"Stop right there." Bryce turned, leaning in, invading her personal space with his bulk and heat. "Nothing about having you here is an imposition. More like a dream come true, okay?"

She swallowed hard as she stared into his eyes. What she saw there had her nodding.

"I don't want you to go, Kae. It would kill me if you left. No matter what happens between us on a personal level, you're welcome here. This is your safe haven too. You'll always be my friend before anything else. I swear that's true." He held his hand out to her. And she took it. "I'm terrified that if I tell you everything, you'll change your mind about letting me open your eyes to what sex can really be like. Part of me wants to be selfish and share that with you before I admit the rest. I know you deserve honesty, though. Enough bastards have taken that from you. I'm not like them. Not like my father. You should make your choice after hearing everything. The crew was trying to convince me not to be a total bonehead before I really fucked things up. They counseled me not to make a fatal mistake with you when they can see it means so damn much to me."

"It does?" She waffled, the desire only growing stronger in her as they spoke of a world full of possibilities she hadn't known existed. She felt like an ignorant noob. And a horny one at that.

"Yes." He squeezed her hand and tucked her close to him as he lay on the bed again. This time she didn't hesitate before curling into his embrace. He held her tight, breathing and organizing his thoughts for a while.

Then he said, "It started with Eli and Alanso. They went out to visit the Powertools crew when those guys were having a rough time. To help out with some insurance stuff after Dave had a serious wreck. While they were there, they walked in on the crew. Sharing. Each other."

"Wow. I can relate." She giggled, trying to ease the tension cording Bryce's thick neck.

"I bet." He glanced down at her and returned her smile. "Except Eli and Alanso apparently stayed. They watched, and maybe fooled around with each other some."

"Well, if I'd known that was an option..." She wiggled her brows, making Bryce grin.

"Such a minx." He pinched her ass, helping her stay focused, though she squirmed. The reaction aligned his thigh with her wet and swollen pussy.

She sighed at the incidental contact.

He grinned. "Okay, maybe this wasn't a bad idea."

"Keep going. What happened next?" She truly wondered—how did a relationship as complex as theirs evolve? Trying to hook up with Bryce alone had nearly freaked her out.

"Well, nothing for a while. Eli was afraid of fucking up our friendship. But Alanso was smarter and pushed him into taking things to the next level. He convinced Cobra to claim Sally too. Thing was, after so long together as a group, it seemed odd for them to exclude the rest of the Hot Rods in their developing relationship, I guess. We were curious about what it would be like between them after being friends so long and what it would mean for our gang. I think at first it was reassuring to have proof that it wouldn't tear us apart. You know, that they weren't going to go off on their own and leave us behind. And well, shit, Kae... It's hot to watch them together. So many of us grew up without really knowing what love was."

She nodded, frowning as she counted herself in that bunch too. Her parents had been hands-off caregivers, her mother drunk or stoned on prescription painkillers until she overdid it one night before Kaelyn had made it to kindergarten. Bryce was the only constant companion she'd had. Until he'd left too.

"To see what was possible when a pair of people, or more, committed to each other. Gave everything—heart, mind, body... It turned me on. Still does, every time. And being included in that sphere of positive energy means a lot to a group of oddballs like us." He paused. "I'm not going to lie to you. I've done more than watch lately. Eli, Alanso and Kaige, they share their women with us. They let the rest of us bring their lovers pleasure—of course the girls have no objections—and know it's an extension of what they can do themselves."

Kaelyn sat up. "You mean..."

"Yeah, I've fucked Sally and Nola. And loved it." He clenched his jaw, closed his eyes for a second, then opened them, searing her with the truth there. "I'd get off on letting Holden, Carver or Roman—hell, all three— pleasure you. Just think, Kae... The four of us, we could do so much for you. Give you more than you can dream of taking. No worries here about polite portions of lust. No stuffy preconceptions about a woman's role in sex either. Take whatever you like. Everything you want and things you find out you desire along the way. You'd be gorgeous as they fucked you. Brought you ecstasy over and over, long after I'd run out of steam."

She shivered.

"You'd do that for me?" she whispered. "You'd enjoy it?"

"Almost as much as I guarantee you would. I mean, you did say you wanted something better than vanilla, right? I think we've got that covered. Boring will not be a word you use to describe a session with the Hot Rods." He stroked her hair, then down her back, his fingers restless as he promised her such a lascivious bounty. "I started doing it because I couldn't have what I really wanted. I'd given up on ever seeing you again, lady. There was gloom in me I couldn't shake. Not even after all that time. I think they saved my life. Sharing was a compromise. One I'd never dreamed possible."

"How so?" She levered up so she could see him in the diffuse light.

"It allowed me to feel close to people. Not alone anymore. Without making me betray the memory of the girl I had pledged my soul to. You, Kaelyn. I didn't feel like I was cheating. Having a girlfriend of my own, someone who'd never be as special as you in my heart. I wasn't lying to them. But it allowed me to find some comfort, some closeness, some *intimacy* that filled the void in a way."

Her heart ached for him. Why hadn't she known he was out here? Hurting? Missing her half as much as she missed him.

"I'm glad you had that, Bryce." She petted him, trying to calm the pulse pounding in his neck. Understanding the emptiness he described, she couldn't blame him for doing something to alleviate it. She hadn't been so lucky.

"It's pretty recent. And kind of developing still," he admitted. "At first Eli and Alanso shared Sally with the guys. But seven on one aren't very good odds."

"That bitch." Kaelyn shook her head in wonder at how spoiled the mechanic had been. Good for her.

Bryce snorted. "Yeah, well, we can be kind of a lot for one woman. And so we started...experimenting. Some of the guys are bi and had been with men before. They sort of bridged the gap. And now, I guess it's becoming kind of a free for all. Like you saw with Roman, Holden and Carver."

"Yeah, they had Carver tied up. It looked like they were doing *things* to him." She would have liked to have played Peeping Tom longer. Still, she blushed when she said, "With a belt and ropes. Wax too. And maybe some toys. I got the impression they were using rough sex to…salve him after this afternoon."

"Really?" Bryce's pupils dilated. "I think he's been pressing Barracuda to play harder with him. I didn't think Roman would go for it, though. He's kind of…dark…sometimes. Especially after any memories today might have stirred up. I think he's still dealing with stuff from his life before Hot Rods. Of all of us, he was on his own longest. Maybe that's why Holden was watching. It's complicated, Kae. We know we can trust each other. Barracuda probably wouldn't feel safe unleashing that part of him unless he knew one of the guys had his back. They'd stop him if he ever crossed the line into unwelcome pain. They'd never let him hurt Meep. So he's free to explore without fear. Only pleasure."

Kaelyn shook her head, awed at the plentiful varieties of loving she'd been introduced to in a single day. So many flavors, and she kind of wanted to try them all.

"I think it's beautiful, Bryce." She kissed him gently. "That you guys have that kind of bond. I'm sort of jealous." She ducked her head when she admitted it.

"No reason, lady." He brought her back for another taste. "I want you at least as much as I want any of them. All of them together maybe. I'd do anything to make you part of what we have. But I'm not telling you that to rush you. One step at a time. For God's sake, you're practically a virgin by comparison."

"Not for long. Right?" She peeked up at him from beneath heavy lashes. "Please."

"I never could say no to you." He kissed her, deeper this time. "And while there might be a lot of firsts today, that isn't going to be one of them. I need to be inside you. Soon, Kae. I'll try my best to make it good for you."

"Thank God," she practically purred as she rubbed herself along his body, tensed now for an entirely different reason. "Otherwise I might have had to go find one of your friends to help a girl out."

"Don't joke. They would do it in a flash." He might have growled a bit as she recalled the way they'd eyed her as she made her way from the bathroom to Bryce's bedroom earlier. A thick, juicy steak indeed.

As if summoned, another knock came on the door. Three hard raps that couldn't be ignored.

"What now?" Bryce shouted, his head falling onto the pillows as he groaned.

The door opened and Holden appeared, looking flushed. Even at half-mast, the bulge he sported made a noticeable line toward his hip beneath the fabric of his sweats.

"They don't need me anymore tonight, but I thought you might have changed your mind." Holden leaned on the doorjamb. "Everything okay in here?"

Genuine concern radiated from the fun-loving man. Kaelyn's heart squeezed as she interpreted his loaded silence as worry, for their future and for his friend. She wanted to reassure him she didn't intend to break up their gang. No calling her Yoko.

"Fine," Bryce answered. Then he added, "Much later, I want to know what went down in there."

His cock jumped, nudging Kaelyn's hip where they were pressed together. And suddenly, she had an idea. It popped right out of her mouth before she could consider, and dismiss it as ludicrous. Or ask Bryce for his feedback.

"Holden, have you ever watched someone lose their vanilla-virginity?" She couldn't say what tempted her to be so bold. Except maybe that she wanted to prove to Bryce—Swinger too—that she could live in their world. Thrive there. Showing off seemed like dipping her toe in their waters compared to what she'd seen and what Bryce had described.

And maybe it was something more selfish than that. Her own desire burned through her, lighting every bit of her on fire. Not one but *two* sexy men focused on her. The thought had her ready to reach between her legs and take care of business herself. Never before could she remember being so needy. Aching so much.

"Nah, I'm kind of a recent pervert. Unless you count the rest of the Hot Rods, I guess. But...is that an invitation?" Holden asked, his pupils dilating at the same time Bryce cursed.

"Kaelyn, no." Bryce tucked her tighter to him. "You should have something soft and romantic. Something fit for a princess. Especially our first time."

"If that's what you think of when you look at me, you'd better get over it." Yanking away, she sat up and put her hands on her hips. "Haven't you been listening to me? I'm not some delicate piece of china. Or a useless decoration."

"You're sure, lady?" He lifted to nuzzle her neck, tipping up her chin so he could stare into her eyes as she decided.

"Yes. Positive." It wasn't a lie. She licked her lips. "I want you to take me. And I want Holden to watch you make me yours. I'm more sure than ever that we don't always get second chances in life. Things you have today could be taken tomorrow. I don't want to waste this opportunity when I know tonight could be the best night of my life. Give me this, please."

"Bring her into our world, Bryce," Swinger encouraged his friend. "Make her a Hot Rod for life."

CHAPTER SEVEN

"He's not joking, Kaelyn. Once you open this door, understand the possibilities, there might be no going back. Being satisfied with less could become impossible. It is for me." Bryce winced. "I don't want you to think that you're not enough for any man, but I can't imagine my life without this bond, without the whole gang. Is that something you could be happy with?"

"I don't know." She didn't attempt to grant him false security. Honesty ruled. "But I'd like to find out."

She wasn't meek or timid. Hopefully he wouldn't mind.

Kaelyn whipped her borrowed shirt over her head, tossing it in the corner. Then she reached for Bryce's pants, tugging on the waistband until he lifted his hips. She wiggled her ass as she peeled them down his muscular thighs and shapely calves, loving the gasps from Holden, who enjoyed her display from behind. She crawled backward until the fabric was free of Bryce's feet and vanquished to the floor as well.

"Are we doing this, Rebel?" Swinger asked.

"Yes. Whatever she wants. Sounds like she's kind of a rebel too." His cock thumped onto his abdomen, the tip painting pearly fluid over his six-pack. "Come in and close the door before there's a whole audience."

Kaelyn shivered. "Mmm."

"You're going to be the death of me, lady." Bryce groaned as she surveyed the length of his erection and tried not to imagine the rest of the Hot Rods packing the room as if they witnessed some virgin sacrifice or maybe an initiation ritual.

Because that was exactly how she felt. Except maybe more like a goddess than an unwilling participant. The appreciation in Bryce's eyes thrilled her. He lay back, letting her explore as she'd never had the opportunity to do before.

Thick, hard muscles were covered in soft, warm skin. She petted him, stopping to flick a nail over one of the hardened discs of his nipples. He groaned and balled his fists in the sheets.

Holden startled her by murmuring in her ear. "If he lets himself touch you, it'll be over too soon. He wants you so badly, Kaelyn. I've never seen him this worked up. But he'll let you take as much as you need. Learn him. Go ahead."

Having someone else to confirm her instincts as she took a new road relieved her rather than alarming her.

Rustling behind her distracted her only for a moment. She peeked over her shoulder to see Holden shedding his shorts. They had to have been uncomfortable with his cock now rigid again.

"Do you mind?" he asked.

"Nope." Knowing she had the power to control every bit of the situation turned her on more. Without a doubt, Bryce would have his friend clothed or banished from the room if she showed an ounce of discomfort. It seemed silly though to make him keep his pants on. An artificial bit of modesty she no longer required.

With Bryce, she could be the woman she'd always longed to be.

He would grant her the freedom to follow her heart. And places farther south.

She squirmed on top of him, rubbing her pussy over his thigh for relief.

"You're gorgeous, lady," Bryce rumbled from beneath her. This time his jaw clenched as he allowed his hands to roam from her knees to her hips. He nearly encircled her waist with his long fingers before reaching up to cup her breasts in his palms. The beaded nipples pressed into his hands, aching for more.

When she whimpered, he didn't stop or ask if she was okay. He knew what she needed better than she did. In an instant, the world flipped around. Bryce rotated them so that her back pressed into his bed and he held himself above her.

"Swinger, brace her so I don't shove her up the mattress." He grunted. "I'm so much bigger than her, she won't be able to stay in place."

"Sure thing." Holden complied. He scrambled onto the bed and put his back against the headboard. He lifted her so that she rested with her head on his abdomen and his thighs bracketed her shoulders. The hot, hard length of his erection pulsed against her neck.

If it weren't for Bryce peering down at her, she might have been tempted to turn her head and take a taste of the man cradling her. Freedom raced through her veins. Anything was possible with them. They wouldn't judge her for stepping outside social boundaries.

For this time, she wanted to focus on the man above her. She hoped it meant something that *he* was her primary Hot Rod. While it might be fun to play with his friends, she belonged to him. Always would.

As if he could read her dedication in her eyes, he smiled before dropping lower. They pressed together, skin on skin, for the first time. Her lids fluttered, struggling to stay open while he swooped in for a kiss.

Tender, liquid glides of his lips on hers surprised her. When compared to the heavy thud of his cock resting on her belly and the bulk of his muscles, his gentleness impressed her. She wondered idly if she'd be able to take all of him. He seemed so big when measured against her body. In proportion, she hadn't realized quite how large he was until now.

A gasp must have given her away.

Holden chuckled behind her. "Yeah, he's a beast, but he won't hurt you. He'll go slow and only give you as much as you can handle."

"I want it all." Stubborn, she might have crossed her arms if they hadn't been busy hugging Bryce to her so she could rub herself against his mammoth frame. "All of you, Bryce."

"You already have me, lady." He kissed her nose then stared into her eyes.

Swinger made himself useful, caressing her upper arms and even the swells of her breasts while she and Bryce lost themselves in each other eyes. He prepared her body for what would come, even as her mind and heart opened to Bryce and the possibilities he presented.

Kaelyn writhed in their hold, straining to get closer to Bryce and his heat.

When he scooted downward, licking around his friend's fingers, then lower, she growled. Her hand flew to his hair and tugged, sharp enough to draw his attention away from her stomach. "No. Not the long way. When you did that before, it was amazing. This time, I need more."

If her face could have flamed brighter, she would have ignited.

Holden cursed softly behind her. "Let him get you ready. He's big. You're going to need to be wet, Kaelyn. The slipperier, the better."

"I already am." She tried not to whine. "Feel for yourself if you don't believe me."

She reached for his hand and dragged it downward. As he leaned forward, he looked to Bryce, who nodded, welcoming the second opinion. When Holden rimmed the entrance to her pussy, she shuddered in his hold, though her gaze never left Bryce's approving stare. Holden's finger dipped inside, causing her pussy to clench around him. But he didn't linger.

"She's soaked." Swinger groaned, then withdrew, popping his fingers in his mouth to sample her flavor. "Don't tease her this time, Bryce. You can do that plenty later. Give the lady what she wants."

"Yeah, what he said." Kaelyn reached for Bryce, drawing him back to her. They fit together perfectly as he aligned their bodies and devoured her mouth. The pressure of his blunt tip on her pussy increased as he flexed his hips, prepared to penetrate.

"Bryce." Holden's stern tone broke them both from the moment just as Bryce's cock nudged at her opening, about to breach her.

"Not now, Swinger." Gritted teeth made the dismissal rough.

"A condom. Here. Put this on." Holden lunged for the bedside table, rocking her torso when he leaned, then held out a foil packet to the other man above her, poised between her thighs. "We've already got one oopsy baby on the way. Let's make sure you plan for your rug rats, huh?"

Kaelyn wanted to tell him she was on birth control, but by the time she could make her brain switch to something so logical, Bryce had already extended his hand toward Holden.

"Shit." Bryce scrubbed his hand over his face then took the protection his friend offered. "I've never forgotten before. But as much as I want to feel you bare, Kae, I don't have it in me to debate about it now."

She agreed a thousand percent. All she could say in response was, "Hurry."

He rolled the latex over his thick shaft, then ringed the base of his cock with his meaty fist. He aimed the head at her pussy and wedged the blunt cap against her once more. This time he didn't stop as he fed his length to her bit by bit.

Kaelyn gasped. She shouted his name as he stretched her channel to accommodate his girth. Her chest expanded too as her heart bulged, tucking him inside in a whole new way, beyond the friendship they'd shared as children.

Behind her, Holden whispered encouragement. He told her she could take it, despite the burn spiking through the bliss of holding Bryce inside her. She leaned into his hold, trusting him to ensure her pleasure, exactly as he had Carver's earlier.

They might be on to something with this arrangement.

Though she'd never attempted tandem sex before, they made it easy for her. Not frightening in the least. In fact, her brain disengaged entirely as emotions barraged her. Her skin came alive. Each nerve ending that was caressed in some way by one of the men bracketing her dropped bombs of pleasure into her system, short-circuiting everything but pure sensation.

"You feel so damn good hugging me like that." Bryce groaned as he withdrew a tiny bit, then invaded her farther. He pressed deeper with every rock of his hips, tucking her into his friend's open arms on each pass.

Holden braced her, helped her accept all that Bryce was giving her. She could never thank him enough for easing her way into things and making sure that both she and her *lover* were satisfied.

A tear slipped from the corner of her eye, horrifying her.

"Rebel," Holden murmured, drawing attention to her emotional overflow.

"Ah, Kae. I'm sorry. Am I hurting you?" He froze immediately, wiping the droplets from her cheek with the pad of one thumb.

"No." She bit her trembling lip then forced herself to reassure him before he withdrew. "I'm...happy. Relieved. I wasn't the problem. It wasn't me. And now I'm not lonely anymore. I'm so thankful I found you today. And your friends too. Fill me, Bryce. Take away the emptiness."

Holden squeezed her, but didn't interrupt her moment with Bryce.

Their rebel kissed her with strong sweeps of his lips and then his tongue. And as he did, the matching advance of his hips granted her wish. His cock felt huge as he tunneled beyond the reaches of even her largest vibrator. He spread her open and filled her up.

Locked together, he took a moment to catch his breath and peer into her eyes with raw adoration and admiration. "You're perfect for me."

"I hope so." She sniffled. "Because now that I've felt this, I think you've ruined me for anyone else."

"Hey." Holden grunted behind her, making her chuckle.

"You *and* your awesome friends," she corrected.

"That's better." Swinger hummed as he rubbed her shoulders, helping her relax so she could hold Bryce more comfortably.

Bryce laughed, making his cock jerk inside her. She groaned and shivered.

He didn't torture her, but instead gave her what she needed by beginning a slow glide in and out. While he made love to her, he kissed her over and over. Between the weight of his body, the sweeping of his mouth, and the incessant caressing of Holden's hands, Kaelyn quickly found herself toeing the edge of a massive orgasm.

Her sheath clung to Bryce's cock, the muscles undulating around him as if to lure him deeper on every thrust. He obliged, fucking her harder as they both lost some of their inhibitions. Holden encouraged them, cheering them on as they raced toward the finish line.

His reassuring hands held her together when she feared she might fly apart in the face of the rapture Bryce bestowed. And when she quaked, afraid to let go and end the most beautiful experience of her life, Holden whispered in her ear, "It's okay. He'll give you more. All of us will. You won't have to wait another lifetime to feel this good. Come for him, Kaelyn. Show him how much you love it."

"Yes!" she shouted into Bryce's mouth.

Bryce didn't have to say anything, his friend having read his thoughts. Instead he smiled down at her as he changed the trajectory of his hips. Long, languid strokes of his cock that sank him inside her from base to tip turned into shorter, faster hammering. He concentrated on grinding them together at the apex of every lunge.

Kaelyn wrapped her legs around him, her heels drumming his tight ass as she forced him as deep as he could go. Though her eyes had drifted closed to savor the sound and sensations he infused her with, they flew open as she felt the first waves of her climax begin.

She stared into his eyes as she obeyed Swinger's urging and shattered.

As if he'd been holding back, waiting for her to tip, Bryce grunted her name then joined her, filling the condom he wore with jets of his seed. A low groan accompanied each twitch of his cock inside her, which set off answering pulses of her own orgasm.

And while they both still shuddered, Holden set her on the mountain of pillows. He crawled over her so that his knees rested on either side of her head and asked Bryce for permission silently.

Bryce glanced down at Kaelyn and read the naked hunger in her gaze. He couldn't back out now, not after promising her a glut of sensation. Despite the rare possessiveness she instilled in him, he seemed to take great pleasure in giving her what she obviously craved.

"Do it," Bryce answered, looking into her eyes long enough to see how aroused she was by his friend's ruddy hard-on.

Holden pressed his cock between her breasts. It slipped there in the pearly precome he painted between her mounds. Bryce assisted by pressing her tits together, cupping his friend with her flesh. A handful of strokes was all it took before Swinger joined them, shooting his release across her belly in several warm spurts.

He collapsed to the side while Bryce shocked them both.

The man still locked inside her hunched his back and lapped at the mess his friend had made, cleaning her and accepting the involvement of his partner. It might be Holden tonight, but it could be any of them next. He quaked between her thighs, his orgasm renewed when she clenched around him, milking the last of his semen from his balls.

She swore she saw the same stars they used to look at together.

They dotted her vision as she shuddered.

And when he finally wilted enough to slip from her, long minutes later, they shared a languorous kiss that mingled the flavors of Bryce and Holden with her own. Kaelyn couldn't help herself. She laughed with delight. And relief.

"Is that a good sign?" Bryce looked over at Holden.

"I think so." The other man smiled slow and wide, wrapping his hand around her ankle and giving it a squeeze.

"I was just thinking...good things come to those who wait." She sighed. "I'm so glad I waited for you to be adventurous. Even if I didn't know that's what I was doing."

Bryce nuzzled her neck, then bundled her in his arms and rolled so that she draped over his still-thrumming body. "So am I, lady. So am I."

He hugged her tight enough to make her squeak.

"Kaelyn," he whispered. "I know this is crazy. We only just found each other again. But you have to know I love you, I always have. And if we keep going down this road, we won't have to go far before I'm *in* love with you."

She tried to say the words back to him, but nothing could make it past her swollen heart. When she lifted her head to meet his gaze, though, she knew he understood. His sleepy smile reflected her own satisfaction. And hope.

As the ringing in her ears died down enough to permit her to revel in Bryce's happy hums and Holden's murmured praise, a scratching came at the door.

Buster McHightops whimpered and tried again to get inside with his master.

Swinger laughed, deep and gravelly. "I guess that's my cue. I'm gonna go clean up and leave you two alone. See you in the morning, lovebirds."

Though he grimaced at the mess he'd made of his crotch, Kaelyn caught something else in his gaze. Something a little sad. She would have reached for him except a moment of hesitation stopped her, wondering what Bryce would think. It was just long enough that Swinger turned away.

The dog yipped, making Holden hurry to admit the puppy before he woke the rest of the house. Except Kaelyn now wondered if they weren't out there in groups or pairs locking the dog out of their own rooms as they pursued similar passions.

She fanned herself at the idea.

Bryce took a breath as if to tell Holden not to go, but he looked down at her, the flowers on the nightstand, and then nodded at his friend. "Thank you, Swinger."

"Anytime." The guy's grin returned. "No, seriously. I'm up for that whenever you'll have me. Maybe next go around I'll help you get those sheets sparkly."

Kaelyn blushed and snuggled into Bryce's embrace. She couldn't believe how much she'd enjoyed sex with this man while his buddy watched on. They *had* made a hell of a mess, tumbling across the bedding, transferring the glitter from her skin to the soft, worn cotton.

It was as if having a witness to the immeasurable pleasure guaranteed it couldn't be fake. Or a dream. It made it more real, and more intense, to share it with Holden.

"Good night, kids." Holden opened the door and slipped out while Buster McHightops bolted inside. The dog charged the bed and flew onto the mattress. Except, instead of crashing into Bryce, he turned circles on Kaelyn's pillow, snuffling in her face until she giggled and scooped him up, hugging him close to her.

"I see how it is, mutt." Bryce grumbled before patting the puppy on his head. "Believe me, I understand."

The three of them snuggled into the bed as Kaelyn's eyes drooped.

Sated. Content. Safe.

She drifted off with Bryce anchoring her to his side—a place she hoped never to leave.

CHAPTER EIGHT

Bryce rolled over, sweeping his arm out in expanding arcs when he didn't immediately sense the heat and softness of Kaelyn by his side. He'd liked it too much when he'd woken up sporadically through the night and found her snuggled up to him. He hadn't been dreaming when he'd watched Holden cradle her as Bryce introduced her to unconventional lovemaking.

She'd looked so beautiful in the moonlight. It was easy to imagine her as some kind of modern Sleeping Beauty. Resisting waking her with a kiss had been impossible.

For someone without a lot of experience, she hadn't seemed to mind his voracious appetite. In fact, she'd surprised him with ravenous hunger of her own, and he'd been only too happy to let her feast.

Cool cotton met his seeking fingers this time. *Shit.* Had she run?

He sat bolt upright, frowning when he noticed Buster McHightops had abandoned the cozy dent he'd made in the pillow near Kaelyn as well. Maybe she'd taken the dog out for a morning walk?

Peering at the bedside clock, he growled. He'd overslept, though not by much. Hard not to when his entire body felt loose and relaxed. The rest of the guys would be taking their turns in the shower and getting ready for the first shift at the garage. They had a ton of jobs on the schedule for today.

Not even the promise of working on Jake Schuller's 1934 Ford could distract Bryce from Kaelyn right now.

He took five seconds to pull on a pair of cotton gym shorts then burst from his room on the hunt. Fortunately, he didn't have to go far or look hard.

As he stalked into the kitchen, he caught lyrical laughter mixed with the deep voices of his fellow Hot Rods. A delicious smell assaulted him as well. Bacon.

His stomach growled.

Sure enough, when he rounded the corner, a hoard of hungry men sat at the concrete island in their enormous open kitchen-dining-living area. They might as well have been a pod of domesticated seals at an amusement park, waiting for a trainer to fling them a fish. They eyed the cook as eagerly as they drooled over the pig belly she fried. And that was saying something. The Hot Rods had an unnatural love for breakfast meat soaked in nitrates.

Bryce included.

"Yo, Rebel. We've voted. It's decided, Kaelyn's staying. Make some room in your closet." Even Mustang got in on the action. Figured—she was as terrible a cook as any of the guys yet enjoyed eating equally as much.

"In favor." Swinger raised his hand fast enough he was in jeopardy of toppling off his stool. No surprise, considering that he'd witnessed the same phenomenal unraveling Bryce had last night.

"You don't have to do all the work, Kaelyn. I'll be your waiter. How about it?" Carver strolled into the kitchen buck naked.

"Did you forget to get dressed?" Roman wondered, crossing his arms.

"I was about to get in the shower, but the smell... Damn, it led me right in here by the nose."

"I don't think that's your nose." Barracuda seemed kind of disgruntled about his roommate flashing himself to the rest of them. *What's that about?* Bryce wondered.

Meep only laughed and flipped his best friend off.

Until he caught sight of Bryce, whose spine had gone ramrod straight. What did he say to make things right?

Was there anything that would suffice?

Carver seemed normal again this morning, if you didn't count the red marks on his ass. He hadn't fooled anyone, he was showing them off. Proud of the advancement he'd made with Roman, and maybe trying to tell Bryce something too.

Had he worked his hard feelings out of his system?

He shouldn't have had to.

Guilt had Bryce clearing his throat as he searched for the right thing to say. Meep was like a brother to him. He couldn't stand to be in the doghouse with the other guy.

"Don't." Carver let his mask of amusement drop for a moment. He reached up and put one hand on Bryce's shoulder. "I don't want to hear any apologies from you, Rebel."

"Shit." Would he ever be forgiven? "I can't say I blame you. I *am* sorry, though."

"Damn. Don't you listen, dude? Sorry for what? For being born to a dickwad bastard who had the chance to give his son every advantage in life but used that power against him instead?" Meep shook his head. "I lost my shit yesterday. I wasn't thinking straight. It's just, well... That was a shock. I always imagined your silence meant you'd had it worse than us all. You know how much it hurts me to imagine what Roman and the rest have gone through. Myself included, I guess. I didn't think about how much more hurtful it would have been to be betrayed by your own father like that. Not at first."

Was it Bryce's imagination or did some color stain Carver's cheeks?

Meep glanced over at Roman, who delivered a grim smile. Bryce stood glued to the floor, with his mouth open, staring at Carver then Roman and back. What the hell had Barracuda done to him last night?

Whatever it was, it had worked. Rebel owed them both, big-time.

He hadn't realized he'd closed the gap between them and hugged Meep until the other guy grunted.

"Hey, I'm a little sore this morning. Go easy on me, big guy." He gave Bryce a one-armed squeeze, then separated them.

"What the hell is this, breakfast and a show?" Kaige burst into their moment before it could get awkward. "Quit your sniveling so we can eat."

"I gotta say one more thing. Then we don't need to talk about it anymore." Bryce cleared his throat.

"No rush, *cabron*. We're only starving." Alanso might have teased him, but he meant the reassurance sincerely, Bryce was sure.

"For so long, I've felt like I had this cancer inside me. I couldn't really tell you guys everything. It was eating me. I felt like I wasn't good enough, because I hadn't been fucked over as much by life. I guess I didn't think I measured up even in the raw-deal department." He paused to catch his breath, afraid to make eye contact with Kaelyn, whose tiny gasp reached him just fine. She might have offered him the solace of her arms if Carver hadn't blocked her passage behind the counter.

Eli jumped in before he could finish. "That's total bullshit. You're one of us, you always have been and you've got the tattoo to prove it. That thing isn't washing off anytime soon so you better get over your inferiority complex."

Bryce swallowed hard and nodded toward their boss and the head of the gang.

Then he faced Carver once more.

"Anyway, I just wanted to say thanks for taking me in and making me yours. From the start. No questions asked." Bryce ran out of gas. "It's meant everything to me. I wouldn't have survived without you guys and the reminder of how strong you all were. If you could get through the day, so could I. I admire every one of you assholes."

"Amen." Swinger slapped the counter with both hands. "Now cook me some breakfast, wench!"

"Hey, don't talk to Kae like that." Bryce found some of that spirit within him as he took a seat at the counter with the rest of the gang.

"Huh?" Holden laughed. "I meant Meep."

Kaelyn appeared to be finishing dabbing the corners of her eyes with a paper towel when he could finally stand to look at her again. Then she was chuckling as Carver sauntered to her side and asked how he could be of service.

"Maybe you should sit this one out. I'd hate for you to scorch your sexy parts." Kaelyn blushed and Bryce knew it was because she found Meep attractive, not because she was embarrassed. The hard tips of her nipples, visible beneath his Hot Rods T-shirt, were a pretty big clue. Her restless shifting from bare foot to bare foot was another as she pressed those long, lanky thighs together in the process. Maybe they could have her for breakfast instead.

"Oh, no worries. I have my uniform right here." Carver snagged an apron they never used from a hook on the inside of the pantry door and tied it around his waist. Unfortunately, that only framed and highlighted his tight ass, complete with decorations courtesy of his wild night. Roman squirmed in his seat.

Kaige reached across the counter, snagged a spatula out of the utensil holder and smacked Carver hard enough to make him jump as he passed by. First shock, then something like desire, crossed his face. He grunted. And then he bent over, stuck out his reddening ass and said, "Please, may I have another?"

"Sorry, but I need fuel first. Hurry up and bring our food." Nova laughed before tossing the utensil in the sink. Nola only rolled her eyes at her boyfriend's antics.

When they returned their attention to Kaelyn, they found her frozen, staring at the exchange. Carver shrugged. "What? You've never seen a man get spanked before?"

"Ummm, nope," she whispered.

"Honey, you're living in the wrong house if you're trying to keep that innocent Goldilocks thing going." Meep winked at her, though Bryce was certain his friend didn't need to persuade Kae to join them on the rowdy side of life. Not after last night.

"I didn't say it was by choice." She laughed when Carver snorted. The sound made it seem as if he believed she could have gotten down and dirty any time she chose. Meep didn't understand where she'd come from or how influential—and intimidating—her father truly was. Men would have treated her as a possession of her father. Only Bryce could really know what that level of oppression felt like. For a moment he was proud he'd granted her an outlet.

His friends would provide others.

From the way she looked at him, she was thinking the same. His chest puffed up.

When Kaelyn dished out her fabulous creation, he realized she'd whipped up a hell of a lot more than simple bacon and eggs. Each plate held an assortment of artfully arranged fresh fruit. From the oven, she withdrew cupcake tins—where the hell had she even found those?—filled with some kind of egg-vegetable frittata-looking thing which she wrapped in the bacon she'd prepared. When it was assembled, quickly and efficiently, it looked more like a sculpture than breakfast. Toast, crusts removed, browned with a geometric pattern across the surface of the bread, finished off her presentation.

As she completed each serving, Carver delivered them with an exaggerated flourish—offset by his still-bare ass hanging out the back of his apron—to each person down the line at the bar. Refusing to miss out, Bryce snagged a plate and prodded the food with his fork but he couldn't suppress the discomfort rising in him. His appetite diminished.

"Holy shit, *lady*." He emphasized the half-joking title as he poked at the meal Meep placed in front of him. "This is a lot swankier than the bowl of Fruity Pebbles I usually chow down on my way out the door. Who the hell are you trying to impress? I thought you understood this isn't how things roll around here. Scale it back, would you?"

"Too much?" She pivoted from her place at the stove and nibbled on her lower lip. "I wasn't trying to be pretentious or anything. It's just that I'm grateful to you all for helping me, for opening your house and *your arms* to me. It meant a lot."

Kaelyn paused, looking from Bryce to Holden while flushing furiously.

"I guess I wanted to say thank you. And maybe pull some of my own weight, that's all." She took her own plate and smooshed the bacon and egg concoction until it was destroyed. The wreckage looked more like generic scrambled eggs after her rearranging. It would taste a million times better, though.

Eli glared at Bryce from his place at the bar. "Rebel, this isn't the time for your prejudices. Pack that shit away. I get now why you might have tried to distance yourself from everything that reminded you of where you came from, but there's no need for that anymore. There never was. Hell, I think most of us would like to be classier if we just knew how. Don't let a bad habit hurt Kaelyn. I know that isn't what you want. But it's what you're gonna do if you're not careful."

Fuck. Cobra was right. Bryce swallowed hard and abandoned his food, although he wanted to gulp it down like a Scooby snack without hardly chewing since it smelled so damn divine. Doubly infuriating since he felt like he'd have to find some fine silverware to do her meal justice.

"I'm sorry, Kae. This is amazing. Perfect." He touched her cheek a moment before leaning in to press his mouth to her parted lips. "You did great. I appreciate having something warm in my stomach before work."

"That's what she said." Holden couldn't help but jump on that one.

Sally smacked him upside the head and shushed him.

Kaelyn pulled away from Bryce's kiss, lacking the pliancy of the night before. "I swear, I wasn't trying to show off or anything.

I wanted to say thank you, and this is what I know. Stuff for parties. Or for my father's guests. I've never made scrambled eggs. But I'll figure it out for tomorrow."

"That's not necessary." His response was curt. Partially because she'd rejected the move he'd tried to put on her and also because the idea of her waiting on them didn't sit right.

"Hey, speak for yourself," Kaige chimed in. "I loved breakfast, Kaelyn, and I'm happy to eat anything you'd like to cook, any time of the day or night. A man could starve to death around this place. I'm getting tired of pizza and takeout all the time."

"You must be getting old, Nova," Alanso teased. "I could eat pizza for every meal."

"I've noticed." Kaige poked his bald friend in the gut. "Careful or you'll start looking like a pepperoni."

Al fought back. "Don't you worry about my sausage. Besides, I do plenty to work it off."

Sally smiled wickedly at her husband and moaned softly.

"Yeah, that too." Alanso reached down and patted her ass. "But I mean real work. It's getting *loco* downstairs. Speaking of... We'd better go open, Cobra."

Eli glanced at his watch, then shoveled more food in his face.

"Maybe I could help out?" Kaelyn offered tentatively. "I'm not sure what I'm qualified to do, but I'm willing to learn. There must be grunt work like stocking stuff, or answering the phones, that anyone can do, right?"

"You're not our indentured servant." Bryce couldn't say why her meek offerings mashed his buttons so much. "Why don't you rest? You didn't get much sleep last night. Stay up here and relax. Maybe have a do over on that bath, minus the sparkle bomb someone planted. That wasn't funny, by the way. Who bought that thing?"

"I kind of liked the glitter-titties look." Holden sighed, confirming the prankster had been at it again.

Bryce threw his napkin at the bastard. He was turned away and so the smack of Kaelyn's hand against his abdomen caught him off guard.

"Fuck you, *Rebel*." She didn't even give him the satisfaction of hearing his name in her haughtiest tone, which probably would have made him hard as a rock. "I'll do as I please. Just because I came to you with my problems doesn't mean I can't look out for myself."

Disgusted, she tossed the rest of her food in the garbage after a single bite.

"Eli, I'm going to introduce myself to your dad." She ignored Bryce as she pivoted toward the head of the garage. "It feels like the proper thing to do. After that, I'll clean up the kitchen. Enjoy your breakfasts, okay?"

"Sure, Kae." Cobra smiled at her. "Make yourself at home. Do as much or little as you feel like. Anything is fine with me."

"Thank you." She kissed him on the cheek, got a wink from Alanso, and Mustang Sally squeezed her hand before she separated herself from the gang and went out the door, shutting it harder than was entirely necessary.

"Way to go, Rebel." Swinger crossed his arms. "Don't fuck this up. I like your girl."

"I bet," Bryce practically growled. "I saw exactly how much you *liked* her last night."

"You invited me in," Holden reminded him. "Is it a problem that I think she's sexy as hell and I can't wait to have a chance to do more than embarrass myself on her fabulous, sparkling rack?"

"Damn it." Alanso pouted. "What did we miss out on?"

Roman held Bryce back. Probably for the best since they didn't have time for a fist fight this morning.

"Only Rebel here reuniting with Kaelyn properly while I watched." Swinger gloated a little, though not enough to be disrespectful. In fact, he seemed awed. Reverent. "She was glorious. And if he chases her away, I might go after her myself."

"The hell you will." Bryce didn't give a shit if all six of the other Hot Rod guys tried to immobilize him, they wouldn't keep him from Kaelyn or from destroying anyone who tried.

If only he'd given himself the same lecture.

"I'm going to hit the shower, then get to work." He rubbed his temples, finished his breakfast in three chomps then stormed off before someone could say something else to make his head explode.

As he was walking away, he heard Kaige mutter, "And I thought *I* was the idiot with the temper."

Bryce had a lot to think about. He hoped manual labor would work off some of his frustration and maybe help suppress the hunger for Kaelyn that pesky pseudo-kiss hadn't done shit to sate.

***

Kaelyn knocked softly on the door to the cute cabin across the driveway from the Hot

185

Rods garage. She was about to search for a doorbell when the door opened and a man who looked a lot more handsome and buff than she'd expected told her to come on in.

"Wow." She blinked a few times. "You look just like Eli. I mean, I know he's your son, but...he's a lucky guy if he turns into you in a few years."

Tom barked out a laugh. "Nice to meet you too, Ms. DuChamp. You're a polite one for sure."

He didn't offer to shake her hand. Instead, he wrapped her in a paternal hug that had her longing to lay her head on his shoulder. As she'd never done with her own father.

"No, she's a smart one. A good eye on her." A middle-aged black woman sat at the kitchen table drinking a cup of tea.

"Please, call me Kaelyn," she said to Tom before turning to his visitor. "But is this a bad time? I can come back. I didn't know you had company and I don't want to interrupt."

"There isn't any such thing as a guest at Hot Rods. I've learned you just make yourself at home. Then you are." The woman stood and shooed Kae toward their gathering before pouring her a cup of tea. "I'm Nola's mom, in case you're wondering."

"Ms. Brown." Kaelyn smiled. "Nice to meet you."

"You too, lovely girl." She passed Kaelyn the simple cup that held a delicious-smelling brew, then nudged a ceramic pot of honey toward her. A spoonful dissolved quickly in the rich amber liquid.

"I wish it were under better circumstances." Tom sighed. "We'd gotten lucky there for quite a few years. It seemed like my kids had put their troubles behind them. And now..."

"I think the universe was waiting for them to be ready. They're grown. They can hurdle these obstacles tossed in their way. You've proved that already, Tommy."

Tommy? Kaelyn giggled inside at how Ms. Brown handled the eldest Hot Rod.

"I guess." He scrubbed his hand through his hair, making his silvery spikes stand on end. "I'd rather be able to take care of it for them."

"You've raised them right. They're equipped to deal with this stuff," Ms. Brown promised him. "Look at Alanso, Sally and Kaige. They're moving on after facing their pasts. The rest will do fine battling their demons. And then everyone can go forward. Happy. Whole."

Though she spoke to Tom, she looked straight into Kaelyn's eyes, broadcasting her message loud and clear.

"She's right about one thing for certain, Kaelyn." Tom cleared his throat. "No one will hurt any of our Hot Rods under my watch. That includes you. I'm pretty sure your dad isn't going to let you go as easily as Bryce's dad did with him. You're a loose end. There's no way for him to explain where you've gone. He doesn't have anything on you to hold over your head like he did Rebel. He'll come for you."

"I know," she whispered. "Should I leave before he gets here? I don't want to put anyone else in danger."

"Don't you dare, child," Ms. Brown snapped. "Let us help you. Tommy's been collecting dirt on Bryce's dad. And yours. They can't be lifelong politicians and never have stepped in it somewhere. We'll find something you can use to buy your freedom."

"I hope so." She swallowed the last of her tea, letting it warm the chill in her core.

More important now, she had to break loose. She wanted to stay. Here. With this amazing family. If they'd have her. At least long enough to come up with a long-term plan. If Bryce wasn't flipping from hot to cold.

He'd scorched her last night. And froze her this morning.

The tea, and Tom's concern, thawed her. Ms. Brown's too.

"It's not only your father that's upsetting you, is it?" Ms. Brown asked softly.

"No." Though ridiculous to spill her guts to near-strangers, they made it easy to confide in them. If the Hot Rods respected these two, she knew they were worthy of her trust. "I'm still in shock that I found Bryce again, I guess. So thrilled. But angry too. Part of me wants to kick him in the balls."

She put her hand over her mouth, embarrassed that she'd admitted it.

"It's a common occurrence around men." Ms. Brown chuckled. "Especially ones you love."

"I don't—" Okay, there was no point in denying that either. She'd loved Bryce since they were children. Except now, she might *love* him love him. Or could pretty easily if she wasn't careful.

"Look, Kaelyn. I'm gonna be blunt. I don't know why certain crap happens in life, especially to good folks. But I wouldn't pass up another shot with the woman I lost if I found out she was still around. Circumstances wouldn't matter a damn. You've got something most people never get. More valuable than a thousand of your dad's estates. Maybe there is such a thing as fate." Tom blinked a few times. "For my sake, give it a chance. Give *Bryce* a chance."

"That's good advice, honey." Nola's mom nodded. "I lost my husband young. Forever ago. It still hurts every day. I know what you felt when you thought your Rebel was gone. But if I had the chance for even one more second with my man, I'd take it. Time is not something you should waste."

Kaelyn brushed tears from her cheeks. She hated that she'd cried so much in the past week. Still, their truth was undeniable. "But he has to let me be who I need to be, not who he thinks I am."

"Those are details. You can work on showing him he's being a dumbass." Tom spoke to Kaelyn, but his hand snuck across his lap to Nola's mom's, as if her words had worked miracles on him too. "When you have that attraction to someone, it'd be a shame to waste it."

The sparks flying between Tom and Nola's mom could have burned down the kitchen. Kae hoped that they took their own advice. Time *was* precious and, if what Bryce had confided in her last night was true, both of these lovely people had spent decades grieving.

Sure, they'd had their families to raise. But now...

"Hell, *Ms. Brown*, I don't even know your name." Tom shook his head with a wry grin.

"But I never asked, and shushed you when you tried to tell me anyway, 'cause it kinda turns me on to call you Ms. Brown."

"Tom! Not in front of the girl." Ms. Brown put a hand to her chest as if scandalized. However, the twinkle in her eyes proved she was teasing. "Wilhelmina."

Tom snorted at such an old-fashioned label for such a spunky lady.

Ms. Brown snorted. "You can call me Willie. I know, I know, joke all you want."

"Willie Brown. It has a nice ring to it." Tom smiled at her, edging closer on the bench seat of the table.

"I think I should leave you two alone." Kaelyn cleared her throat.

Tom didn't seem to notice as he stared at Nola's mom, leaning in slightly until Kaelyn wondered if he was going to kiss the pretty older woman right then and there.

"You come back any time, you hear?" Tom spoke to Kaelyn, though he didn't glance away from Ms. Brown. "My door is always open for you or any of the rest of my kids."

"*Our* kids," Ms. Brown corrected.

"Thank you, Mr. London."

"Tom, remember?" he corrected, finally peeking at her with a devilish grin that reminded her a lot of Eli when he was near his soul mates. "And by 'my door is always open', I mean, unless it's shut. Just for a little while."

"I've waited too long for this to last 'a little while'." Ms. Brown harrumphed then rested her palm on Tom's cheek lightly so he knew she was only teasing.

"*O*-kay." Kaelyn laughed as she wrinkled her nose in mock disgust at the mushy display from the Hot Rods' parental units. She normally wouldn't have risked being rude to someone she'd barely met, but they'd put her completely at ease. She couldn't wait to torment Nola and Eli with their parents' escapades. "I'm going back to the house to take care of the mess I made of the kitchen. Then I guess I'll be in the garage. Thanks for the chat."

"Anytime." Nola's mom repeated the offer this time. "Like...in a few hours. Come back this afternoon if Bryce still needs a kick in the pants."

Tom chuckled. Kaelyn hadn't gotten the door closed entirely when he swooped in and seemed to be doing one hell of a job kissing Ms. Wilhelmina "Willie" Brown silly.

CHAPTER NINE

Kaelyn stacked invoices in a wire basket she'd dug out from a bin behind Eli's desk, then used an old, stained cloth to dust the surface, now that she could see the whole thing. She perched on the chair behind it to admire her work. She liked sitting in the big leather monstrosity that was part of the head mechanic's workspace. It looked like it'd come out of a fast car.

Probably had.

She taped a label to the bin then started organizing the already paid portion of the paperwork into folders she'd created by vendor. How they'd gotten anything accomplished in this sty left her baffled. Their skills under the hood must have been superb to compensate for the messy business side of things.

Alanso sauntered in from the garage, probably looking for his husband. Or his wife. Or maybe both. *"Joder, chica."*

Spanish wasn't a requirement to understand what he meant when he froze and winged a glance from the bare desktop to her then to the filing cabinets. As she looked around her, she hardly recognized the office from its previous clutter to this afternoon's tidiness.

"Um. Is it too much? Did I go overboard again?" She nibbled her lower lip as she considered what the place had looked like earlier this morning when Eli had rummaged around for a piece of paper. In need of something to do, she'd volunteered to search in his place. It'd taken her hours to unearth the receipt for a part he needed to exchange. So she'd gone ahead and started rearranging. The change was drastic, but she'd had a lot of nervous energy to work off.

"It's awesome. If Bryce doesn't keep you, the rest of us will." He winced when she didn't laugh. "If Mustang was here, she'd have smacked me for that, I think. I didn't mean it like your face tells me it sounded. He's not *loco* enough to let you go, *chica*. Don't trouble yourself with that."

How could she not let him off the hook when he tried so hard to reassure her? Kaelyn grinned. "I know what you meant. Anyway, I don't care what Bryce thinks. I'm just hoping this is helpful. I like to straighten stuff up. I'd be glad to work the front desk while I'm here. You know, take appointments, log shipments, do the billing, check people out...stuff like that. Help however I can. I'm not looking for a handout."

"First with the fancy cooking, and now this..." He smiled and patted her on the shoulder. "You're going to be a huge help around the shop. I've felt worthless in my life before, Kae. You're not. Not at all. Each of us came here with nothing. You're no different than any of us. Just need some time to land on your feet. You're doing a good job of it already. Cut Rebel some slack, huh? My guess is he's afraid you'll see working as a step down. He doesn't have the greatest impression of rich people. I sort of understand why now. Not that I think he's right when it comes to you or anything."

"What?" She sniffled as she stood. Could that be true?

"I can speak for myself, Al." Bryce must have been listening at the door for a bit. She hadn't heard it open. He stepped inside and softened his rebuke by buffing the mechanic's bald head before dropping his hand on Alanso's shoulder, where tattoos hugged his bulging muscles on either side of a white sleeveless shirt that tucked into his unzipped coveralls. "But you're not wrong. Mind if I take it from here."

"Go ahead, *cabron*." Alanso shook his head. "I was screwing that to hell. I'm glad Cobra, Sally and me are out of those woods. Less talking, more fucking, that's the way to clear up this *mierda*." He mumbled to himself in Spanish as he wandered out into the garage and left them alone to work out their issues.

"Sorry, Kaelyn." Bryce grimaced.

"For what? Barging in here, your friend's crassness or for trying to put me up on a pedestal?" She couldn't help her bitter almost-shout.

"That last part." He shrugged. "You're going to have to get used to the guys and their dirty mouths, sorry. I don't think I can train them any better than I can Buster McHightops, who pissed in Nova's boot again this morning. And frankly, nothing is off limits to the Hot Rods or to you. So I'll damn well show up whenever I like, often if you're around."

He paused, though not long enough to give her an opening to speak.

"I'm sorry that I didn't think about things from your perspective. I've held a grudge for a long time. Against my dad. And yours. For the way they use the power of their money, their positions. I forget sometimes that not everything from that life is…"

"All show, no soul?" She understood completely, and hated that he'd lumped her in with the rest even for a moment.

"Shit. I'd never think of you that way." He rubbed the back of his neck. "More like I felt for the first time in a long time like I, and what I have, wasn't good enough. It pissed me off. And I was afraid."

"Of what?" She tipped her head as she read the genuine concern in his eyes.

"That I don't deserve you. That I can't keep you the way you're accustomed to living." He sighed.

"First off, you can't *keep* me at all." She had to get this straight right now or she'd leave in the car they'd repaired earlier and never look in the rearview mirror, no matter how much of her heart she left behind. "I'm my own woman now. I won't belong to anyone else."

"What if you take me instead?" He sauntered closer, perfuming the air around her with the scent of man and motor oil.

"Then I'd be the richest girl in the state." Kaelyn smiled.

"I'm yours. If you still want me. Dumbass moments and everything."

She went into his open arms and rested her cheek on his chest, right over the flaming patch that held his name embroidered on it.

He squeezed her tight.

"This is what I want, Bryce." She hugged him back, reveling in his solid embrace. "You're all I need. You, a place where I can be myself, take what I need and contribute meaningfully to the people who…"

"Who what, lady?" He stroked her hair from root to tips, which landed barely above her ass.

"Who will be my new family," she whispered. "I feel it already, Bryce. I could belong here."

"Damn straight." He lifted her up and she locked her legs behind his back so they were eye to eye, then lips to lips.

Their kiss escalated until the thick length of his cock rubbed her mound and she moaned into his mouth.

"Hold that thought." He looked around, kind of guiltily. Did he care if the rest of the Hot Rods caught him making out during shop hours? "I came in here to ask if you wanted to do something with me."

"There are zillions of naughty things I want to do with you. But I get that's not what you mean." One more stolen kiss would have to hold her. It wasn't like him to act like this.

Now that his past was in the open, he didn't seem to have any secrets from his garagemates. "What's going on?"

He nuzzled her neck, close enough to whisper.

"Kaige is going to pop the question to Nola tonight. He's got some elaborate thing set up. When we went out at lunch, it was to help him pick out a ring. The Powertools crew is even coming. They're on their way now. I can't wait for you to meet them. Would you help me with my part? I have to pull off some dumb dance and lip synch. Plus, I thought...."

"Yes?" Her heart melted as she watched his cute factor shoot through the roof.

"I'd like you to be part of it. With the rest of us." He cleared his throat. "If I haven't totally fucked things up with you, I think you should be there. Celebrating the future with us. I want you to be one of the gang."

And that was the best pledge she'd ever heard.

"Of course. I'd love to." She sighed. "But Bryce, are you going to keep me locked away somewhere? If that's what you expect of me, to be arm candy and wait all day for you to come home and fuck me... I can't do that. I'm not that woman anymore. Promise me, you won't do that to me."

"Son of a bitch." He let her down gently then smacked his fist into the filing cabinet she'd finished sorting through so recently. "Is that what you think?"

"Isn't that what you said? That you didn't want me dirtying my hands?" She stood akimbo, daring him to deny it.

"Yeah. Damn. I guess I did, but I didn't mean it like you're thinking. I want you to have the life you're used to. The standards you're accustomed to."

"Bryce, think about what you're saying. I'd willingly trade a life of luxury for one of love." She watched her words sink in. "Isn't that what you've done yourself? I don't want fancy things or to waste my time on idle pursuits. The only thing that's important to me is you. Us. Maybe the Hot Rods, if they'll have me too."

He rushed to her and swung her in circles. Thankfully the desk had been cleaned off or he would have scattered months of paperwork in a hurricane twisting around them. "I'm so sorry, Kaelyn. I didn't mean to underestimate you. I swear. I only wanted to give you what you need to be happy."

"I said it before, and I'll say it again. Every day until you believe me. I already have everything I need. As long as I have you." She stared up at him. "Don't stifle me, please. Like with Holden last night, the freedom you gave me… It means everything. I thought you understood."

"I do now. I won't take that away from you. And after Cobra sees what you've done in here, I'm pretty sure he's not going to let you off office duty for the next fifty years. Sorry for your luck." He grinned then rested his cheek on the top of her head.

"Okay. Why don't we go upstairs and figure out what to do so that your part of Kaige's proposal kicks ass?" She wondered if they might fit in some make-up sex too.

"*Our* part, lady," he corrected her.

When he hauled her into his arms, shouted that he was taking a break as he marched them out of the open bay, then leapt up the stairs three at a time, she figured they were finally on the same page. No one seemed surprised by their departure. In fact, she thought she saw Sally clapping and bouncing from her perch on Tom's front stairs, where she was chatting with Ms. Brown.

***

Later that evening, they stood in the twilight, hand in hand.

Bryce had parked his white Rebel AMC, complete with blue and red stripes, in the lot

201

around a bend in the road. After a quick make-out session in the backseat of his car, they'd traipsed to their mark, a few trees behind Nola and a few trees in front of Mike—the Powertools crew's foreman—and his wife, Kate. They had their adorable little girl, Abby, with them as well. After they were finished here, Kaelyn intended to play with the toddler and her equally adorable buddy, Nathan, who belonged to another of the couples.

The nine friends who'd joined the Hot Rods' scheme made Kaelyn feel like she'd inherited a whole network of people in a single day. They accepted her as part of Bryce. Not questioning their bond, which had reformed in an instant. Suddenly she felt wealthy beyond measure.

Crisp air proclaimed the coming fall. Scarlet leaves rained around the dirt road they stood on the side of, waiting for their cue. Buster McHightops sat near their feet, looking preposterous yet dapper in a doggie tux. A top hat with slits for his ears perched at a jaunty angle, completing the look.

Kaelyn took stock of Bryce in a nice pair of jeans, the first ones she'd seen him wear that didn't have tears or a prominent grease stain. A navy plaid button-down shirt only enhanced his rugged beauty. She scanned him from head to toe before licking her lips.

"If you do that again, they're going to find me nailing you to that tree over there when they come by. Which should be any minute now." He wrenched his stare from her to peer down the lane.

"It's been a looooong time since last night." She loved that she could make him yearn the same way she did.

"You should have let me return the favor earlier." Bryce crossed his arms, putting her off-balance at the sight of his strong forearms beneath the unbuttoned and rolled-up sleeves of his shirt.

She licked her lips again as she remembered how he'd tasted and how full her mouth had been of his heat and hardness when she'd seduced him into letting her try her hand—or mouth, she supposed—at a killer blowjob. At least she figured she'd done a pretty bang-up job for her first try. It hadn't taken long before he'd begged her for release. Assuming control, reducing him to the bundle of neediness she'd been the night before had reaffirmed her decision, and granted her power she'd never experienced.

The mixture had been potent enough to make her feel drunk on it.

And she couldn't wait to do it again.

"As much as I love that deviant look in your eyes, it's show time. Here they come."

Bryce took her hand and seemed to be counting under his breath.

"Relax, Bryce. You were always a great dancer." She remembered how watching him or swirling around the ballroom in his arms was the only fun part of the tedious events they'd attended.

"It's been years since I waltzed." He shook his head. "Are you sure this is the way to go?"

"It's going to be perfect. Look, they're starting!" she shout-whispered, though Kaige and Nola were too far away to hear.

Kaige's Chevy Nova came crawling into view. The windows were rolled down and Bruno Mars' "Marry You" spilled from the vehicle. As Kaige inched along the lane, people began to jump out from the hedges on the side and sing lyrics to Nola, who had her hands in front of her face and appeared to be laughing or crying—or both.

Each new verse was delivered by someone important to her. First Eli, Alanso and Sally. Her mother and Tom danced across the road while singing in perfect tune. Then her sister threw petals in the air as she continued the song. After each group was featured, they joined the parade of singing, cheering friends making their way down the lane in an ever-growing procession.

Kaelyn found herself holding back tears of her own as Bryce whisked her into his arms and they twirled along to the music with Buster yipping at their heels.

She was surprised when they merged into the crowd escorting the Nova. She looked up to see a woman with a microphone, which was surrounded in a box-shaped ad for the local TV station, trailing them—a videographer right behind—along with a gathering of random people who must have been out for an evening walk before catching on to the sensational proposal unfolding in the park. Lucky break for the station. They must have been filming something nearby.

Kaelyn ducked her head, hiding in the crook of Bryce's arm as they relished the squeals coming from the passenger side of the Nova as the Powertools crew continued to enhance their celebration. By the time the song ended, Kaige had pulled his car next to Bryce's Rebel and the rest of the Hot Rods' hot rods.

He climbed from the vehicle and opened Nola's door. She barreled him over when she rushed from the vehicle and pounced on the gorgeous man, making his dreads swirl around them. He cushioned her so that she landed on top of him, his hand over her still-flat stomach.

And then he set her down and got on one knee.

The words he spoke were low enough to be private, but the looks on their faces told the entire story. The cute news reporter rushed past Kaelyn, bumping her shoulder as she snuck in for a close-up. Holden stepped up, preventing the woman and her cameraman from intruding too much on the precious moment.

Then no one had eyes for anything but the pure bliss radiating from the couple, who embraced before Kaige slid his ring on Nola's finger. The group of friends and family surrounding them cheered in support of their everlasting promises.

Together, they led the way to the pavilion Nola's sister, Amber, and Kaelyn had rushed to prepare for an informal engagement party. No way would the Hot Rods let their Powertools friends leave without enjoying every bit of their company.

It was the most perfect moment she could ever recall, watching the couple blossom while Bryce held her close to his warmth and the pounding of his heart, which she could measure against her cheek.

He looked down at her and smiled, then covered her lips in a delicious kiss that neither of them was in a rush to end. So what if they were the last ones to dinner?

It was worth it.

***

Kaelyn tidied up some white lights that had drooped from the tree branches and surveyed the apothecary jars filled with punch, which sat on the lace tablecloth that draped a picnic table. At least they *had* been full. It seemed people were enjoying the fruity concoctions.

Same could be said for the appetizers that had been scarfed down before moving on to the cupcake bouquets and the plates of cookies.

"I can't believe we pulled this off." Amber high-fived Kaelyn.

She clapped hands, then went in for a full-on hug.

"We make a good team." Her smile was genuine. When was the last time she'd been part of anything bigger than herself?

"Yeah, we do. Your *hors d'oeuvres* are amazing. Those gorgonzola pear tartlets are going on my catering menu for sure." Amber laughed, then stopped, growing very serious. "You know...my sister ditched me for this lot."

She waved toward the Hot Rods. Kaelyn could see that she was happy for her sister, but maybe a teensy bit worried too. "I have a ton of events coming up, stuff I hadn't even told Nola about yet since she's been so preoccupied."

"Do you need help?" Kaelyn was glad to pitch in.

"More like I need a new partner." Amber's eyes grew big in the twinkling lights. "You'd be perfect. I mean, I don't know what you're planning to do..."

"Are you trying to steal my admin?" Eli sauntered over, one arm flung around Sally's shoulders. "I just got her."

"Oh, you're working for Cobra?" The pretty mocha-skinned woman tried to hide her disappointment, but Kae could tell. She was flattered.

"Part-time, anyway. Maybe I could do half and half?" She nibbled her lip, wondering what Bryce would say. "I do love setting up events. It's something I actually have oodles of experience with."

"I can tell." Amber smiled. "You'd be a huge asset to my company. It wasn't Nola's favorite aspect of our collaboration. She was more into the marketing and consulting side of things, but...I think this is what I like best. And now that it's just me, I can take some new and different clients. Steer the business in a more specific direction. What do you say? Would you be my part-time partner? I'm willing to settle for joint custody."

"Hey now, that's what I like to hear." Holden planted a smacking kiss on Amber's cheek. "A woman who shares. Perfection."

"Eww, Swinger." She swatted at him. "Not like that. Not when my sister's in the picture."

Kaelyn, Eli and Mustang chuckled at their antics. But when Amber refocused, Kaelyn knew it was the right thing to do. She put out her hand and shook Amber's. "I'm thrilled to accept. Thank you."

"Sweet!" Amber rushed forward and hugged her. "This is going to be great. I can't wait to tell my mom. Have you seen her?"

"I think she's over there by the tree swing." Kaelyn pointed to where Tom pushed Ms. Brown lightly in an arc while she dangled her bare feet and her dress rippled in the wind.

"Oh, jeez. I'm surrounded by hopeless romantics." Amber pretended to be put-out, but Kae caught her soft smile.

"I'm afraid you are." Bryce rejoined the group along with Nola and Kaige. He stared right at Kaelyn, his gray gaze lasering into hers with an intensity that had her checking her watch. How much longer until they could be alone?

Or slightly less than alone, but in private.

She counted the seconds.

"Rebel, I think you should know I hired your girlfriend. Meet my new partner in crime." Amber grinned.

"Seriously?" He looked to Kaelyn. "That's great. I still can't believe you two did such an awesome job with short notice. Everything looks phenomenal."

His praise warmed her from the inside out.

"Thank you." She went onto her tiptoes to kiss him. "You don't mind me taking a job, really?"

"Absolutely not." He hugged her tight. "I'll support you in whatever you want to do."

"Even…" She whispered a wicked suggestion into his ear.

"Definitely." He shouted over to his friends. "Kae and I are going home. See you guys there."

They laughed and teased him about his eagerness, but he didn't seem to care.

"Congratulations," he said more seriously when he turned to Kaige and Nola. "It couldn't happen to better people, truly."

"We could say the same." Nola hugged first Bryce, then Kaelyn.

And while they rushed back to Hot Rods, they missed Holden intercepting Sabra Harp—the local news reporter—after she'd interviewed the newly engaged couple about their spectacular proposal. Bryce and Kaelyn hadn't thought to remind anyone to make sure they were kept out of the footage when it was shown as a feel-good piece on that night's news.

Swinger did it for them, looking out for his own.

CHAPTER TEN

Kaige took Bryce aside as they entered their apartment. "Do you think Kaelyn's ready?"

"For?" He took a deep breath.

"Tonight won't be the same if we can't celebrate *our* way. You know, start the rest of my life as I intend to live it." Nova had never seemed so earnest before. "Tom and *Willie*—I still can't believe that's her name—are gone for the night. The Powertools crew had to hit the road, though I wish they could have stayed too, and I'd really love to share this once-in-a-lifetime experience with you guys. Kaelyn included. You're not going to let her go, are you?"

"Never," Bryce confirmed.

"Then we have to test the waters sometime, right?" Kaige cleared his throat. "Unless you don't imagine yourself sharing anymore."

That wasn't an option. Not for Bryce and not for Kaelyn.

He couldn't believe how much their needs aligned.

Complementary decadence.

"No, you're right." He glanced over to where Kae chatted with Nola. She was sandwiched on the couch between Holden and Carver without seeming the least bit intimidated. In fact, she seemed to be leaning on Swinger a bit as she talked to Kaige's fiancé about embarking on a partnership in the event-planning business with Amber, Nola's sister.

Things were working out even better than he'd hoped.

Speeding along, exactly like he preferred.

Only one thing left to try.

"Let's do it." Bryce clapped Kaige on the shoulder. "If she doesn't want to or can't handle it, I'll take her out, but I want you to know that I'm happy for you and I want to celebrate with you."

"Maybe someday soon I'll be doing the same for you when Kaelyn agrees to be part of us officially. I know you'll make it happen when the time is right. After you've adjusted to finding each other again." Nova smiled. "She's perfect for you. And for us."

"I'm going to do my best. If she'll have me. I have to give her some time to figure things out, though. Stand on her own before I take that from her by making her mine." Bryce sighed. He could wait if he had to. She was worth it.

"She will." Nova sounded certain. "I'd bet my car that she's loved you since you were kids. Same as you have her. I remember how I'd find you staring at that picture of her you have in your room sometimes. I knew I recognized her, you jerk."

"Usually on her birthday. It was the hardest thing to know another year had passed and she'd probably forgotten me a long time ago." Bryce could finally confess to his friend.

"Nah. Bonds like those don't fade away. You could leave here for ten years and you'd always be a Hot Rod, right?" Nova shrugged. "Not that I ever want you to try it..."

"I'm not going anywhere. And if I have my way, neither is she," he promised.

"Then let's go party, Rebel. There's a lot to be pumped about." Nova grabbed his crotch. "And he's extra happy anticipating it."

"I can see that." Bryce laughed at the hard-on Nova didn't bother to shield from him.

"You want to talk to her first?" Kaige winced as if the delay would be painful.

"When it comes to this, I think it's better to show than to tell." He shook his head. "She got an eyeful of Carver, Holden and Roman the other night. She knows everything. It won't be a surprise."

"Okay, I'll follow your lead when it comes to her." Nova nodded. "I'm really happy for you, Rebel. Nola's the best thing to ever happen to me. I'm glad you have that too. That we all can drink it in."

"Same goes, Nova." Bryce hugged his friend. "I can't wait to spoil your kid. I bet we can Hot Rod a tricycle."

"Ah, shit. I'm going to be a dad." He laughed and looked slightly horrified at once.

"We'd better pack in all the fun we can before then." He tipped his head toward the living room and the rest of their gang. "Come on."

***

Kaelyn could sense Bryce approaching the instant he turned his attention to her. Every nerve in her body went on high alert as if he was a magnet and she a great big pile of iron shavings.

Mustang Sally took one look at the intensity on his face, and Nova's, and grinned. She did a fist pump, then whipped her neon pink tank top off. She sported a leopard-print bra beneath that made the best of her assets.

"How did you know we weren't going to ease Kaelyn into this?" Eli shook his head at his wife as he laughed.

"Because she doesn't need kid gloves." Sally shrugged, then allowed Alanso to peel her jeans from her voluptuous hips.

"Good point." Nola nodded before allowing Kaige to make quick work of her dress.

"Thank you." Kaelyn figured, what the heck? She might as well be proactive. With a shimmy, she shucked the borrowed jeans Nola had lent her, then tossed her blouse over the sectional couch.

Bryce glanced from her to his friends. The men and women focused on their partners, or for those single...on her.

She shivered.

"Are you scared?" he asked her. "We don't have to do this."

"I'm more afraid that if I don't, I might never know what I'm capable of. What it feels like to really fly. I've had by-the-book. Dull. That doesn't cut it. And if what I felt with you and Holden last night is any indication, taking on four guys is going to blow my mind." Kaelyn grabbed his collar and tugged him lower so she could kiss him. They stayed that way for so long most of the other people in the room were stark naked the next time she peeked around.

"If it's too much we can slow down. Or watch. Say the word and I'll put on the brakes. No one will be upset or offended. Okay?" He kissed her softly, letting her really decide.

"Yes. But I'd rather you step on the gas." She unbuttoned Bryce's shirt, loving the hard expanse of his chest, which she revealed with each fastener she undid. Tracing the valleys between his six-pack abs, she pushed the fabric aside until it fell from his shoulders.

As if the balmy air from the fireplace hitting his bare skin was some kind of catalyst, he sloughed the rest of his clothes and divested her of her underwear in no time flat.

Suddenly, she was surrounded. Bryce, Holden Roman and Carver paid her an inordinate amount of attention. Kissing and touching every inch of her as they told her over and over how glad they were that she was joining them.

They pressed on her shoulders, guiding her to the floor until she lay in the middle of the four gorgeous men. Bryce kissed her as his friends plumped her breasts, suckled the taut peaks and one of them—Carver, she thought—pressed between her legs, spreading her thighs around his shoulders and petting her trimmed pussy.

A cry flew from her parted lips into Bryce's mouth. He broke contact for just a moment from where he lay beside her to observe his friends. "Go ahead, Meep. Eat her pussy. Get her good and slick for me."

Kaelyn whimpered when the Hot Rod did as her man ordered. She realized in the first instant his mouth fused to her and began to ply her with wet laps and suckles that he was part of Bryce. An extension of the man she adored.

Bryce was giving her this. More than he could ever do alone.

It was a phenomenal gift. Precious and rare.

She appreciated it. Him.

And she let him know with the ferocity of her hunger as she devoured his mouth.

"That's right, lady," he whispered against her lips when they broke apart to drag air into their burning lungs.

She heard a moan from the couch above her. It drew her attention for a moment. Sally was held tight between her two men, watching as the four guys on the floor taught Kaelyn what it was like to experience their brand of unconventional loving.

Kae smiled at Mustang, wishing she could flash the woman a thumbs-up, but her hands were otherwise occupied, exploring the men who treated her so well.

Then she returned her attention to them, urging them to escalate their feathery touches so that she could really soar.

"Not so fast, lady." Bryce tsked at her, distracting her again with another slow assault of his mouth on hers.

She sank into the floating feeling that enveloped her, allowing the talented manipulation of Carver's mouth between her legs to arouse her beyond anything she'd felt before. Kaige's pledges of everlasting love—the ones he made over and over to Nola—seeped into Kaelyn's consciousness, and she knew the rest of the guys felt the same way.

About each other. About the women who'd joined them.

About her.

Overwhelmed, she lost control of her restraint. An unexpected orgasm washed over her. Carver buried his face in her folds and sipped wetness from between them.

"Why don't you let Bryce get to work over there?" Roman suggested to his roommate. "Besides, I want to taste her on you. Come here, boy."

Meep obeyed without complaint. He pressed a goodbye kiss over her mound then hustled to Barracuda, who grabbed Carver's face between his hands and began to lick the glistening stubble that covered his chin.

"Fucking delicious." Roman groaned as he fisted his own shaft.

"I can't wait to taste her again either." Bryce groaned as he eyed her pussy.

"Oh no." She wriggled, grabbing for his shoulders. "I want you inside me. Please."

"I'd never be able to resist begging like that." Eli reached into a fishbowl on the coffee table, which she hadn't noticed before, and tossed a condom to Bryce. Cobra sank onto the couch and tugged Sally into his lap. "In fact...why don't you ride me, Mustang?"

She happily obliged, lifting up so he could fit his cock to her and slide home. They sighed together as Alanso beamed, watching them please each other.

Bryce must have been as moved as her. He hummed, then pressed against her with the fat tip of his covered cock. She relaxed, letting him work his way inside her.

"*Yes,*" she hissed. While he stretched her, easing as far as he could reach within her rippling sheath, his friends added fuel to the fire. They stroked her hair, ran their hands over her bare skin and even massaged her feet until her toes curled at the overstimulation.

"Bryce," she moaned. He took her cue and began to move, with liquid glides that seemed impossible for someone of his size and stature. His cock caressed her from the inside out, always slow and steady, keeping the next level just out of her reach.

After enduring it as long as she could, she attempted to meet him stroke for stroke and increase the pressure.

He dropped lower, pinning her to the floor, making movement impossible.

"Bryce!" She practically screamed his name. Except out of frustration this time.

"Yes, lady?" He paused, going even slower, drawing out her torture.

"Stop treating me like I'm going to break." She pointed to Eli, who had tipped his wife onto her hands and knees on the couch. He fucked Sally hard and fast from behind. He knew she was strong enough to take what he was giving. Heck, to enjoy it. "Like that. I want it like that."

"Kae, you're not ready yet. You'd never even had two guys before yesterday, never mind four, for Christ's sake. Let me keep things sweet and slow for you. There's enough extra going on to overwhelm you if we're not careful." He swiveled his hips, which felt divine. Unfortunately, it wasn't enough.

"If you can't fuck me like I want, get out of the way and let one of your friends do it for you." She wrapped her legs around him and rolled. If he hadn't been so surprised, she surely couldn't have flipped him. Perched on top of him, she took advantage of his momentary daze.

She dug her fingernails into his pecs and rode him, forcing his thick shaft as deep as he could get within her. Tipping her head back she shouted, "Yes!"

Roman came behind her and wrapped her hair around his wrist. He kept her in position as she took advantage of Bryce's cock—no, his whole body—to finally rub the ache inside her as hard and fast as she needed.

"That's right, Kaelyn. Take what you need. Use him until he wises up and gives it to you." Roman smiled down at her, reveling in her debauchery.

Grateful, she leaned over and took Roman's cock into her mouth, sucking on the tip of his erection, or more depending on where she was in her circuit, fucking herself on Bryce. Having them both, tasting one while squeezing the other, spurred her on. Holden must have knelt beside her because his steady hands cupped her breasts, pinching her nipples and keeping the bouncing from becoming uncomfortable on the oversensitive mounds.

"Carver, get over here." Barracuda ordered his roommate to do more than stare while tugging on his full cock. "On your hands and knees."

He did as asked, with his ass facing Roman, as if preparing to host the other man. Kaelyn shuddered, eager to see Meep get fucked too. Instead, Baraccuda laughed. "Not just yet, boy. The other way. Kneel over Bryce. Lick Kae's clit. Make her come on Rebel. Show him how lucky he is to have a passionate woman like her begging him to pound her tight, wet pussy."

"Oh, God." Kaelyn lost her grip on Roman's shaft as she cried out. It was impossible not to when he talked dirty like that. Bryce grunted as her pussy clenched around him. His hands kneaded her waist, encouraging her to take him faster, harder. Finally.

From the couch, Alanso cursed in Spanish. She peeked over to find him watching them. He left Sally's mouth and rounded behind Eli. "I need to fuck, Cobra."

He bit the head mechanic on the shoulder, then rubbed his cock in the valley of Eli's ass.

Cobra leaned forward, lying over his wife as he spread his legs and made room for Alanso behind him. Kaelyn didn't know if it was the image of him penetrating his husband's back passage or the first glancing touch of Carver's tongue on her clit that did the trick, but she flew into climax before she could prepare herself. This compared in no way to the quick, gentle releases she'd given herself in bed at night. Or worse, the fake climaxes she'd acted out with Montgomery.

Kaelyn felt untamed for the first time in her life.

She didn't care about her hair tangling, the perspiration coating her skin or the unrestrained moans that burst from her lips, which were wrapped around Roman's cock again—when had that happened?

The only thing she focused on was pursuing the ecstasy flowing through her.

"Don't stop." Holden urged her to continue, his hands along with Bryce's keeping her in motion. He included Carver in that directive too. "Keep licking her, Meep. Get her off again. It's got to be hard to concentrate with Bryce sucking your cock and balls like that, but you can do it. Focus."

Kaelyn didn't think it was possible to shatter so completely then spiral upward again immediately. She was happy to be wrong. So wrong.

They made her come several times in a row, until her thighs quivered around Bryce's powerful hips, which now lunged upward to meet her every downward plunge. Holden braced her. One of his hands still plying her breasts with naughty caresses while the other rested on her neck. His powerful chest pressed to her back, helping her keep the pace and position that brought her so much pleasure.

But when she came again, they must have realized how noodley her limbs had become.

"Enough," Roman told Carver, his declaration punctuated with a slap on Carver's ass that had him scrambling off Rebel.

"Swinger, help her down." Bryce surrendered his grip on her waist and allowed his friend to cradle her. He lay on the floor on his back and pillowed her on his chest.

She sighed and gasped for breath.

"You didn't think you were done, did you?" Bryce grinned as he towered over her, coming to kneel between her thighs as well as the spread legs of his friend. "You want to be mine, to take the full extent of my passion. It's yours. All yours."

Kaelyn shuddered when Bryce tapped the head of his cock against her clit several times. He rubbed the thick crown around her pussy until she was surprised to find her opening kissing it, trying to pull him inside.

"That's right, lady." The title seemed out of place given the circumstances. Yet, in some ways, she'd never felt as privileged as she did now. She glanced to where Kaige and Nola had tuckered themselves out and keenly watched the show she and the four men surrounding her put on.

Even Alanso, Eli and Sally seemed to have slowed to observe the new coupling.

Bryce growled at his friends. Somehow it felt more significant than a bit of voyeurism. She knew that after this, they'd be bonded. She was becoming one of them.

"You're gorgeous, Kaelyn," Bryce murmured to her.

"Take a picture, it'll last longer," Kaige ribbed from the couch where he snuggled Nola, still buried deep inside her. "Or I will for you, if you want."

Before either of them could object, he dug his phone from his pocket and snapped a shot. He laughed. "Oh shit, I really took it. I was just going to mess around. Too bad, you look super hot, Kae."

His thumb hovered over his touch screen, prepared to delete the damning image.

"Wait!" Kaelyn lurched, making both Bryce and Holden groan as she jolted against their pulsing cocks. "Don't."

Suddenly she wanted to see herself. This new her. And have a reminder always of what she could become if she let herself embrace the woman within.

"Seriously?" Roman smiled down at her. "That's hot, Kae."

"Hell, I'll even video you if you really want." Nova angled himself for a better line of sight. "No one here will judge you. We each have our own kinks."

Nola smiled up at her fiancé, clearly approving of his acceptance.

"You're sure about this, lady?" Bryce tucked a damp strand of her hair behind her ear as he hesitated giving Kaige the nod he seemed to want from his friend.

"Yeah." She glanced down, then decided it was far too late for modesty. "I want proof that this isn't some crazy dream. And that...this can be me. The real me. Whenever I want."

"I didn't think I could find you any sexier." He bent over to cover her mouth with his in a tender kiss, at odds with the way she'd ridden him minutes ago. And those simple swipes of his lips over hers were all she needed to get riled again.

Okay, maybe the camera had something to do with it.

"You heard the lady," Bryce said to Kaige then turned back to Kaelyn. "Let's give him something to record for posterity, huh?"

"She's so damn wet, Rebel." Holden groaned from below her. "I'm getting soaked down here. Fuck her already. And maybe I can join you?"

"Are you asking me or her?" Bryce looked at Kaelyn for a verdict.

Her brow knitted as she wondered what exactly they were proposing.

"There are a few ways. If you were prepared, I'd let him fuck your perfect ass," Bryce rasped. "But you don't want to jump into that without some...advanced play. I could let him fuck your pussy from below. We could take turns."

Kaelyn whimpered at that idea.

"Or we could take you together," Holden proposed. "You're drenched. I bet you can hold us both."

"I'm big enough." Bryce shook his head. "I won't hurt her."

Kaelyn smiled up at him, thrilled that she could trust him to test her limits yet not push beyond them. In the Hot Rods' arms, she could explore safely. Nothing had ever been so attractive.

"Take turns," she told Holden. He didn't waste any time complying.

"Yeah, let him in, Kae." Bryce finished rolling a condom over Holden's length, then guided his friend's cock to her pussy and slipped him inside. Though he wasn't as thick as Bryce, he still felt plenty good. The angle of his penetration ensured he rubbed her just right.

"Thank goodness I'm on birth control," she murmured, then turned to Nola. "I can see how you forgot. I have a feeling I could too one of these times."

"Mmm. They're good at distracting a girl. But I only ever let Kaige have me bare. And just that once. Though I suppose now there's no reason we shouldn't..." She practically purred as Kaige began rocking into her again slowly, though he still held his phone up, focused on them.

Bryce toyed with Kaelyn's clit as Holden rocked into her from below. Rebel bent down to kiss her.

Ever helpful, Carver came to her side and helped lift her shoulders. He supported her neck so she could reach better. Bryce made out with her while Swinger fucked her. He grunted and cursed as he triggered the clenching of her pussy, which hugged him even as he worked to tunnel inside her harder and faster.

"Rebel, don't you think Meep deserves a reward for eating her while you fucked her?" Barracuda knelt behind his roommate, playing with the piercing in Carver's taut nipple.

"Yeah, Bryce, let her suck Carver's cock while you and Holden fuck her," Sally suggested as Eli ground into her and Alanso pumped into Eli. "I always like that."

"Plus, then Roman can fuck Carver." Nola's sexy voice seemed even deeper and huskier than usual. "I love watching them do it."

Kaelyn tightened around Holden, coming with a quick, hard release that had the man below her shouting and writhing. Her convulsions pushed him from her body before he had a chance to shoot within her.

Bryce nipped her neck, then placed his thumb in her mouth. She sucked it while he took Holden's place, filling her to capacity once more. She moaned, releasing his digit. Within seconds, Carver had nudged Bryce's hand aside and offered his cock for her enjoyment.

Kaelyn smiled up at him and opened her mouth, inviting him inside. Suddenly shy, he said, "Thank you."

Then he took her up on the offer.

He made a pleasant mouthful, something to suck as Bryce rocked her in Holden's warm hold. A bed of muscles below and the press of Bryce above lulled her as she drew on Carver with steady, rhythmic pulls.

Roman stroked Carver's ass and ran his hands along Carver's tight abs, crooning praise to the smaller man as he sidled up behind his roommate. A *snick* of a cap drew Kaelyn's attention momentarily as Roman prepared his lover's ass and his own cock, slicking them both.

She could sense the instant hardening of Meep's shaft between her lips—going from stiff to steely in the blink of an eye—when Roman breached the tight ring of his anus.

The first lunge Roman made into Carver pressed his roommate's cock deeper into her mouth than he'd been, and she choked. Bryce was there, immediately, his palm on Meep's stomach, keeping him from feeding her more than she could handle.

She glanced up at him and he met her gaze, smiling. Well, kind of. His features were twisted somewhere between exhilarated and cautious. She'd take both.

Kaelyn relaxed, letting the men surrounding her choreograph their pleasure. She was along for the ride and enjoying every second. This time when she came, she was careful not to scrape Meep with her teeth. Again, Bryce tapped out, letting Holden take up his place.

"If we don't switch again, I'm going to explode." He groaned.

"I need a new condom, this one busted." Holden waved toward the ripped latex she'd ground against with her lower back while Bryce pounded her.

"I said I'm on the pill." Kaelyn stared at Bryce, letting him prescribe their course of action. Could he tell she didn't want to wait even a moment longer than necessary to be filled again?

"You heard the lady." Rebel winked at her. "I think she's getting greedy for your cock, Swinger. Better give her what she wants."

"Honestly, I'm not going to make it much longer myself." Swinger gasped as he reentered her with a single fierce stroke, this time naked. "I almost lost it the last time she came. She's so fucking tight. Hot as hell too. And like this... Jesus."

"I know." Bryce stared down at them, his hand peeling off his own condom then lingering to stroke his erection slowly and surely. "Go ahead, Holden. I'm dying too."

His admission made Kae shiver again with lust. To know she could affect such sexy, veteran lovers thrilled her.

"Can I come in her, or do you want me to pull out?" Swinger asked between thrusts.

"It's up to her." Bryce shrugged as she peeked up at him, his friend's cock making it impossible to answer.

Except with her body, which spasmed around Holden. She couldn't stop herself from coming at the idea. It was like a chain reaction now, making her peak again and again before she ever fully stopped.

Roman plowed into Carver, making her rock as she sucked him harder to keep his cock in her mouth. He began to groan and curse until she wondered if he'd join her soon.

"Rebel, I'm gonna—"

Kaelyn shifted her hips to grind down on Swinger as he tried to retreat. She took him deep inside her and held him as he unraveled. Searing blasts of his come pumped into her in time to his shouts and the squeezing of his arms around her as he called out her name.

Carver joined his friend, filling her mouth with the proof of his pleasure, which she swallowed before she drowned. Roman groaned, long and low, and mirrored his roommate, as if savoring the clenching of Meep's ass around his cock.

Before she could come down, bombarded by the decadent sights and sounds around her, Bryce urged Holden to withdraw. He slipped from her, allowing a trickle of fluid to run from her body. Bryce praised her as he fitted himself to her and slid home, much more easily this time, lubricated by his friend's release.

Carver and Roman lay beside her, bracketing her with their warmth and roaming hands as Holden held her for Bryce to fuck. Except she knew it was more than that. Her rebel made love to her, surrounded by his friends.

Their friends.

These men would never let anything happen to her. She was free at last.

Cherished.

Bryce laid butterfly kisses on her mouth, nose and eyes before touching his lips to the dampness she was surprised to notice on her cheeks. He melded them so completely she knew they'd never be apart again.

Steeped in the support of so many people who cared for her, especially the man inside her, she let go completely.

Kaelyn surrendered to rapture. She heard Bryce shout her name and moan over and over as he flooded her with his come. Though she couldn't find the words to respond to his unspoken declaration, she knew he could see their future in her stare, which he never once glanced away from.

Ruined—for the night and forever, if it didn't contain regular sessions with these men—she allowed herself to be lifted into Bryce's arms. He held her close as he settled them in front of the fireplace and whispered a million amazing promises to her before she crashed, completely exhausted, into a deep and peaceful sleep.

CHAPTER ELEVEN

The next day, the Hot Rods reveled in utter laziness. Content, they hung around the living room, lost in their own pursuits. Some watched a movie together, a couple played games. The women spent hours browsing the Internet for wedding dresses they thought Nola would look amazing in when she walked down the aisle.

Tom and Willie stopped by, holding hands while they checked in on everyone. None of the Hot Rods seemed to be able to stop themselves from calling her Ms. Brown.

Even Buster McHightops sprawled on his back in his doggie bed and took a ridiculously long nap instead of running around like his usual maniac self.

It was a peaceful Sunday.

Kaelyn could spend every weekend for the rest of her life exactly like this.

When the movie credits rolled, the guys watching TV flipped over to the local channel.

Holden sat up as Sabra Harp read off some human interest stories. Kaelyn raised a brow at Bryce, who seemed to notice too. He grinned back at her.

"Sudden interest in current events, Swinger?" Bryce ribbed their friend.

"My money's on the sexy newscaster," Eli joined in. "I saw how you chased her down at the engagement party."

"I was trying to make sure she didn't air any footage of Kaelyn and Bryce," Swinger spat out, obviously annoyed that they'd made him reveal his worries.

"Is that why you've got a boner right now?" Kaige gathered his dreads.

"No. That's because she's smoking hot," Holden admitted. "And I really, really hate to say this…"

He pinched his nose between his fingers and took a breath.

"What?" Bryce gathered Kaelyn to him as if he sensed danger.

And he was right.

"I looked online a while ago." He cursed. "They didn't edit you out. Not all the way. There were some shots where you guys were in the background. I wish I could spank her for that."

With a growl, he flicked off the TV.

"So we need to be prepared." Eli stood, pacing behind the couch. "It's only a matter of time before they find you."

Kaelyn hated that the day had been ruined. Because of her.

No, because of her father. And Bryce's.

The last of her reserve slipped away. "I'm done waiting. I'm not going to give other people that kind of power over my life anymore. I'm going to him. Them. I'll finish this myself."

"As long as you don't think you're going alone." Bryce gripped her hand so hard she winced. "Sorry, sorry. Shit."

"Do you think you can keep your temper under control if you come too?" She closed her eyes. "We can't give them any more ammunition."

"Why does this sound like you have a plan?" Nola wondered.

"I've been thinking about it a lot. Especially today." She sighed. "I can't risk you all. Or your child."

She cut Kaige off when he began to deny she was a risk. He shut his mouth, torn when she played the baby card.

"We'll go on the run if we have to. I did it once. We can do it again." Bryce turned to her, tucking her hair behind her ear. "Maybe we should take that trip through Europe I promised you."

"You can't give up Hot Rods. This place means everything to you." She swallowed hard. "I know you don't want to hear it but if it came to that, I *would* go alone."

He cursed, but she put her hand over his mouth to smother his sputtering.

Alanso laughed at her bold move.

"I don't think it'll be necessary." She took a deep breath. "I need you all to know that I didn't cook up this craziness until this morning. What happened last night was spontaneous. And genuine."

"What the hell does that mean?" Roman whipped his head toward her.

"I can use the pictures and videos Kaige took last night...sort of like reverse blackmail. We can beat our fathers at their own game." She looked up at Bryce. "They manipulated you with photos of me. Got you to leave with threats of making them public."

"Lady, you have to know I didn't give a shit about being seen kissing you. I wasn't worried about me. I tried to protect you from the shame my father was going to—"

"Shush." She kissed him lightly. "I understand. But think about what we have now. There's no way in hell my father would want the photos of last night made public.

What if the video...of us...leaked? It could destroy his career. Your father's too. Especially if it came out that you'd never actually done all that charity work overseas after the support people gave him and his campaign in response."

"Those photos are for us. Our eyes only." Bryce started to turn an unhealthy shade of purple. "They're something beautiful. I don't want to use them like that. No way will I flash them to the world. I won't expose you...or the Hot Rods."

"Rebel, listen to your lady." Eli strode to their sides. He put a hand on each of their shoulders. "It's a genius solution."

"You want everyone to see what we have? To belittle what they don't understand?" Bryce shook Cobra off and stood.

"It'll never come to that," Kaelyn promised. "Maybe you've been gone too long to remember. But image is everything in politics. To our fathers. They'd never risk it. Let's fight fire with fire. We can get a lawyer. Draw up an agreement. I'll relinquish my right to my inheritance and agree never to contact them again if they'll do the same and leave us to live however we like. Out of the spotlight."

For a while no one said anything as they tried to find some pitfall.

No one did.

"Are you sure this is what you want?" Bryce swallowed hard. "This life? Me? There won't be any going back after this, lady. We do well for ourselves. I'm not as wealthy as your dad though. Or mine. Not even a fraction of that."

She huffed. "Why are we talking about this again? Money doesn't mean crap to me. It never bought my happiness before. Besides, I'm going to make my own way with Amber."

"Don't forget about your office-manager job," Eli nearly shouted, as if she'd change her mind. "You'll be in charge of payroll. Give yourself a nice salary. A raise too, for having to work for such slobs."

Mustang Sally laughed out loud, shaking her head at Rebel.

"Of course I'm sure, Bryce. I've dreamed of this since we snuggled together in the tree house. Well, not *quite* like this. But the important parts. Or are you saying that because you have doubts? It's happened so fast. If you don't want to be tied to me yet—"

"Okay, now I'm going to slap you." Nola rolled her eyes.

Eli clinched the deal. "As the boss, I'm officially offering you that position. And inviting you to move in with us and our psycho puppy. You're part of our family. If you want to be."

"I do." She sniffled.

"Let's go tell Tom and Ms. Brown." Bryce yanked her into his arms and squeezed her so tight she could hardly breathe.

"Uh, Rebel…" Carver interrupted. "Maybe you'd better call first to make sure it's safe. I think the days of busting through the door unannounced might be over. Tom gives us the same courtesy. It's the least we can do."

"Ack!" Nola slapped her hand over her eyes at the same time Eli made a sour face.

"Good idea, Meep." Bryce laughed.

***

Two weeks later, the waiting room of the law office of Lance Silver overflowed with seven muscular, tattooed badasses, three women, two parents and one dog, who'd refused to be left at home alone. The Hot Rods gathered around Kaelyn and Bryce, insulating them from the pair of assholes who'd filed through the mahogany door in three-piece suits.

Bryce refused to think of them as their fathers.

After a decade apart, he was relieved to feel…nothing…when the men strode past him without a word.

He fisted his hands, wishing he could do more than sign some contract to make them pay. For Kaelyn's sake.

"Settle down, son." Tom spoke low enough to avoid being overheard. "Keep your eye on the prize. Nothing matters but walking out of here a free man, with your girl."

Rebel nodded, then enfolded Kae's hand in his.

She looked up at him and smiled. Though it was partly bravado, her faith was the only encouragement he needed.

Together they faced the men that had nearly torn them apart.

With the slash of a pen that probably cost as much as his Rebel AMC, the two bastards signed away their rights. And the hope of ever seeing their children again.

Though obviously furious at being outwitted, they seemed relieved rather than upset to be getting rid of baggage. Bryce looked to Kaelyn as her father walked out without a single glance in her direction.

"Goodbye, Dad." Tears filled her eyes, and she whispered, "Thank God it's over."

He nodded and kissed her cheek, afraid to do more when they both were so on edge.

Then she ran to Tom and Ms. Brown, who wrapped her in their arms as she sobbed.

By the time the whole gang trundled up the stairs to their apartment above the garage, thankfulness had taken center stage over the grief they'd deal with in time.

All of them, except Nola, took a sip directly from the bottle of champagne Tom cracked open in their kitchen before they parted ways.

Tom and Ms. Brown went back to his house to comfort each other, while the Hot Rods did the same.

Together, they could heal each other. They always had and always would.

EPILOGUE

"**S**o are you finally going to take *your* car for a drive?" Kaelyn dangled the keys to the Maserati in front of Bryce a few weeks later.

"You know, that thing is fun, but I think it's better suited to you, lady." He looked her up and down. "Sleek, fast, elegant, and purrs like a kitten. It always reminded me of you. I think that's why I liked it so much. It's *your* car now."

Kaelyn laughed as she patted his chest. "Nothing says you can't have both, *enjoy* both. The Rebel for your badass side and a luxury car for cruising. Bryce, it's not wealth that made our fathers the way they are. I don't believe that anyway. And I hope you don't either. You're not the kind of man who'd act like a bigot. Don't make those generalizations. Stop letting it color your view of the world."

Bryce actually grimaced. "I guess I deserve that. It was easier than believing the evil I saw was really part of my father instead of greed or corruption because he was filthy, stinking rich."

"Well, now you know better. So come on, take me for a ride." She wiggled her brows and tossed the keys to him, which he caught deftly with one hand, embracing their pasts so they could move on with their future.

"Now that's an offer I don't plan to turn down...ever. I know a great place we could christen this baby." He scooped her up and whirled her around until the rotation, or maybe him alone, made her dizzy with delight.

Bryce set her down softly at the passenger door of the Maserati. "Unless you're still feeling sore? You know like last night how you said you couldn't because—"

He said it quietly, but Holden still must have heard the fib she'd told Bryce the prior evening to keep him from seeing... The jerk snorted from the car in the bay next door where he was installing pretty peach leather seats with black piping. Kaelyn darted over and smacked his ass.

"Don't ruin my surprise!" She laughed when he jerked upright and banged his head on the roof of the car.

"Well, you might have done that on your own." Bryce was suddenly beside her, turning her to face him with those broad hands on her shoulders. "What kind of trouble are you up to?"

"It wasn't my idea!" Mustang Sally shouted from the back of the garage as the Hot Rods gang began to gather around them. "I only held her hand."

"Why am I getting the feeling that you, Nola and Sally didn't exactly hit up the mall after work yesterday like I thought?" Bryce rubbed his chin and narrowed his eyes.

"Because we didn't." Nola stepped closer, with Kaige right behind, his arms looped around his fiancé's belly, his hands splayed protectively there. "But you can't get mad at a pregnant lady."

"No fair." Bryce faux-pouted, though he'd confessed last night how much he secretly loved the developing friendship the three women shared. "Are you going to make a habit of teaming up on us guys?"

"Yep," they answered in unison, then giggled as they glanced from woman to woman.

"Oh, fuck us." Eli shook his head while Alanso laid his hand on his husband's shoulder in sympathy.

"Put him out of his misery, Kae," Holden suggested while Carver and Roman joined them, completing the circle of friends and lovers. "Show him what you did so you two can get laid again and quit staring at each other with those googly eyes."

"A little help?" she asked Holden as she turned so that her back was to Swinger. With a flick of her fingers she unbuttoned her jeans, then drew down the zipper.

"Uh, lady? Here? Now? The shop is open. And so are the doors." Bryce had the whole crowd chuckling with his sudden modesty.

"Don't worry, I'm not getting freaky. Want to show you something." She shimmied the tight denim off her waist and lower, as Holden made sure she didn't scrape the bandage or the healing patch of flesh beneath it. His hands warmed her against the cool almost-autumn air.

The discomfort of tape being peeled off her skin had her glancing over her shoulder at Swinger, who grinned. "Looks good from here."

"What—" Bryce's wonder had his eyes widening when she spun around and put her new tattoo on display.

"I hope you don't mind." Suddenly Kaelyn found it hard to get more than a breathy whisper through her throat. "I didn't mean to be presumptuous. I know you all have one because you're part of this place and each other. I guess I got it to be more like...a fangirl."

Bryce dropped to his knees behind her. He cupped her hips in his hands easily and leaned forward, kissing the unmarred tissue beside the art on her bum. The Hot Rods logo was surrounded by swirling text. An *A* above, then *Hot Rods*, and finally *Rebel* beneath it.

No matter what, she'd spend the rest of her life embracing the rebel spirit she shared with Bryce.

"Well?" She began to fidget. Holden came closer, hugging her when he noticed her unease while Bryce studied her behind.

"I love it, Kaelyn." He rose and turned her toward him while Holden took care of her, recovering the tattoo and putting her clothes back in order so she didn't have to look away from the man of her dreams.

She swallowed hard as he gathered his thoughts, or maybe wrestled his emotions so he could continue.

"And I hope, someday, you won't doubt your rightful place. Here. You're one of us, lady. And now you'll never forget it." Bryce laid his palm over her ass and squeezed gently. "You're mine."

"And we're yours," Holden murmured behind her. "We've got your back. Always."

"My heart too." She sniffled before she whispered her promise in return. Her gaze flickered from Hot Rod to Hot Rod and the women they loved. She respected, admired and adored them all, each and every one in their own way.

***

"Excuse me." Someone cleared their throat in a manner too obvious to be natural from the doorway. "Is anyone around?"

Holden spun, closest to the intruder, and crossed to them in a flash. The rest of the gang surrounded Bryce and Kaelyn, protecting them as they got their shit together. Or, actually, as they shared a deep and passionate kiss.

Swinger was pissed to have missed the action, a sealing of the oath they'd just made each other. A moment he'd come to anticipate after each person had joined their group. At least, he felt imposed on until he saw who had approached.

That damn reporter, Sabra Harp, stood with her hands on her hips, attempting to peek behind him at the poignant exchange she had no business spying on.

"What do *you* want?" he snapped. Partially because he was still pissed she'd aired the footage including Bryce and Kaelyn. Mostly because he had watched the news every single night since then to get a glimpse of her

252

pert lips and flashing blue eyes. Her voice alone had the power to make him hard. A feat he hoped she wouldn't perform with him standing in front of her.

Shit. Fuck. Damn.

"First, I came to apologize." She met his gaze straight on, unflinching. "I know it doesn't matter, but I told my producer they couldn't use the clips of Kaelyn and Bryce and to cut it out. At the last second they decided the emotional impact of your friends celebrating was too good for the editing-room floor. I didn't know they were going to put it in the piece it until it was too late."

"Yeah, but you handed over the recording to them. With every bit included." Holden couldn't help but lean forward. He told himself it was to be more aggressive, not to catch a whiff of that tangerine scent he'd noticed the last time he'd bumped into this vixen.

"I know, and for that I'm sorry. I trusted them. I shouldn't have." She glanced away. "Anyway, I don't work there anymore."

"Yeah, right. I saw you on the news last night." Holden probably shouldn't have admitted that.

"You did?" The edges of her pretty lips tipped up at that.

"Oh, yeah" Roman piped up to bust Holden's balls. "Swinger here is a regular broadcast addict lately. Didn't know you were that concerned with current events."

Behind his back, Holden gave his garagemate the finger. A couple chuckles broke out.

"Well, anyway… I gave them two weeks' notice, then quit." Sabra sighed. "I thought I should come by in person and tell you how sorry I am that my bad choice put you in danger. I didn't realize the full repercussions until I got your—uh—*blunt* email. I'm honestly sorry."

Kaelyn came up beside Holden and reached out to the petite reporter, enfolding her in a hug, which the woman looked like she might desperately need right then. "It's okay. Don't worry about it anymore. Everything worked out. I've made my own share of bad decisions, especially when it comes to believing people who don't deserve your trust."

"No one here is innocent." Eli strode forward, every bit the King Cobra they knew and loved. "I've hurt people I cared about. Deeply. It's how you make it up to them, and how you go forward that counts, Sabra."

"Thank you." She flashed a wan smile and a few blinks of her watery eyes up at Eli as if he were her hero. And somehow that made Holden...possessive.

Uh-oh. Oh no. No way.

Time to get this woman out of here before she could do any more damage. He liked his life just fine the way it was shaping up, thank you very much. The last thing he needed was some woman screwing with his head. Or places below the belt.

"And what else?" Holden wasn't buying her sudden U-turn. The woman could have emailed him or called him anytime to apologize. She had his business card and the Hot Rods website, including his contact info, was a quick Google away.

"Swinger." Carver issued a low warning and touched his elbow. He tried to settle but couldn't with Sabra this near him and the people he loved.

"I have a business proposition for all of you—" She paused and whipped her stare to Holden when he growled. Then she stood straighter, put her shoulders back and said in a rush, "I've done some research. And, well, since I'm currently unemployed, I have an idea. Something I think could be big. And it involves you guys."

"We're not interested," Holden barked.

"Let the woman speak, Swinger." Eli's command silenced him. As the garage owner he had every right to listen to some dumb sales pitch if he wanted to. And, yeah, maybe Holden was overreacting to Sabra. It seemed every part of him did.

He willed his cock not to harden, but it didn't pay him much mind.

Carver slapped Holden on the back. "Come on, I bet this is going to be good."

But no one expected her to say what came next.

HOT RODS
"HOLY SMOKIN' MÉNAGE!!!!"
Guilty Pleasures Reviews
SWINGER STYLE
JAYNE RYLON
NEW YORK TIMES BESTSELLING AUTHOR

She's running on empty...and he's ready to fill her up.

After watching his mother crumble in the face of heartbreak, Holden believes monogamy is bull. New week, new woman, that's just how he rolls. Too bad one taste of Sabra Harp leaves him salivating for more.

Sabra was ready for the climb from local news reporter to national anchor—before her pursuit of a story almost destroyed the Hot Rods, whose friendship she has admired from afar. Too bad they all hate her guts. That's okay, she despises what she's become too...enough that she's just told her boss where to stick it.

When Holden drives a drunken Sabra home and puts her to bed, her blatant invitation almost has him following her between the sheets. She's willing to let him take charge in bed, friends included—and he's willing to listen to her amazing business proposition, which could rocket the Hot Rods to stardom.

Yet as his friends have paired off, Holden realizes that to participate in their polyamorous games without becoming a third wheel, he needs Sabra. And she needs him...oh, how she needs him.

EXCERPT FROM SWINGER STYLE, HOT RODS BOOK 5

"Do me a favor, okay?" Sabra couldn't take anything else today.

"Sure." Holden scrubbed his hand through his hair then over the beard stubble she wanted to rub against like her cat when it smooshed its face against the corner of the couch in a compulsive display of scent-marking.

"Don't talk to me. I can't argue right now. Now with you or anyone else. Shut up and drive. Fast." Sabra knew she was weak where this guy was concerned. His disgust had prompted her to resign. Shameless, she licked her lips as she scanned him from head to toe. Unruly hair, a strong jaw and a mouth that was quick to curve into a crooked smile—complete with dimples—for the right person. Badass prep defined his style. A soft, worn hoodie covered a Henley. A navy and gray wide-striped scarf somehow only made him look sexier instead of dorky. Trim and fit, she bet he had more definition than it appeared beneath his clothes. Jeans tattered by work and genuine wear versus a fashion factory hugged his perfect ass and framed his package just right. If he lingered, she might make another request of him. One she would regret in the morning. Like so many other things that had happened in the past twenty-four hours.

"Can do." He didn't ask for permission. Instead, he simply plucked her from the ground and swung her into his surprisingly strong arms. Within seconds, he'd used her fob to unlock her car, whisked her toward the vehicle that lit up in response, then deposited her gently on the passenger seat before rounding the hood to join her.

"Lincoln and Town, above the pizza shop," she instructed as if he were a cabbie instead of a hot-rodder.

Sabra leaned her head on the window and tried not to catch glimpses of his capable handling as he quickly rearranged the mirrors then pulled onto the dark street, heading toward her apartment.

Why the hell did he have to choose now to reappear in her life?

She ignored the stinging in her eyes and the part of her that would love to unload on him. To confess what she'd done. Try to make amends. Or use him to erase the pain ripping her apart. Truth was, she didn't deserve him after what she'd done. It wouldn't be fair to either of them to cross those lines, tangling pleasure and pain, reminding them both of what had happened. Because of her.

When they pulled into the alley behind her apartment, she didn't know whether to be relieved or sad at how quickly they'd gotten there. It took her three tries to find her door handle. He appeared outside, opening it for her and hauling her from the vehicle before she had her shit together.

Pathetic. Why couldn't she do anything right around this man? And why did she want to prove to him that she wasn't as lame as he assumed she was?

He wrapped an arm around her waist and practically carried her up the stairs. At the top, he used the only other key on her ring to unlock her apartment. When he attempted to usher her inside, she stumbled over the threshold, ending up plastered full-length against him.

Heat flared through her core. Before she could think better of it, she'd coiled her arms around his neck. With that much contact, she had no hope of resisting the magnetism between them. Instead, she fused their mouths. He didn't shove her away.

Several heartbeats pounded through her as Holden returned the kiss with interest, making her toes curl. If the world hadn't already been off kilter, he'd have tilted it on its axis. His taste, the suave seduction of his mouth on hers and his palms cupping her ass all combined to fire her up.

He inched forward, then pivoted, trapping her against the door jamb. His hands pinned her wrists over her head, and his body held her still as he plundered her parted lips.

Sabra let him take, allowed him to use her and guide them both through blazing pleasure. Her nipples dug into the firm heat of his chest. His hard cock nudged her belly as they strained toward each other.

She gave herself into his care and he rewarded her trust with rapture.

Until he yanked backward. She nearly fell on her ass without his support.

"Damn you." He banged his fist on the doorframe above her head, making her jump. "That isn't what I came here for."

"S-sorry." A flush stained her cheeks. How much mortification could one woman withstand in a day?

Quitting before she could get fired for insubordination had sucked. Holden's rejection was twice as bad. "Really. I screwed up. Everything."

Before he could reach out for her or bash her again—his disgust wounding her much more than fists ever could—she tucked inside

and closed the door, locking him out of her
home.

And her life.

ABOUT THE AUTHOR

Jayne Rylon is a *New York Times* and *USA Today* bestselling author. She received the 2011 RomanticTimes Reviewers' Choice Award for Best Indie Erotic Romance.

Her stories used to begin as daydreams in seemingly endless business meetings, but now she is a full-time author, who employs the skills she learned from her straight-laced corporate existence in the business of writing. She lives in Ohio with two cats and her husband, the infamous Mr. Rylon.

When she can escape her purple office, Jayne loves to travel the world, SCUBA dive, take pictures, avoid speeding tickets in her beloved Sky and—of course—read.